# STEPPING SIDEWAYS

## WORLDS OF STEAMPUNK & DYSTOPIA

*Stepping Sideways: Worlds of Steampunk & Dystopia*

Edited by Emily Larkin &
Lynne Stringer, 2024
Stories are © to individual authors

Cover Layout by Carmen Dougherty
Layout by Rhiza Edge

978-1-76111-178-5

Published by Rhiza Edge, 2024
PO Box 302,
Chinchilla QLD 4413
Australia
www.wombatrhiza.com.au

All rights reserved. No part of this publication may be reproduced, stored in a retrieval system or transmitted in any form by any means without the prior permission of the copyright owner. Enquiries should be made to the publisher.

# STEPPING SIDEWAYS

## WORLDS OF STEAMPUNK & DYSTOPIA

EDITED BY
**EMILY LARKIN &
LYNNE STRINGER**

# CONTENTS

**FOREWORD** . . . . . . . . . . . . . . . . . . . . . . . . VI
    LYNNE STRINGER
    EMILY LARKIN

**BIG TOP BREAKOUT** . . . . . . . . . . . . . . . . . . . . 1
    LYNNE STRINGER

**MECHANICAL MAGIC** . . . . . . . . . . . . . . . . . . 20
    LINSEY PAINTER

**LENA OF THE AIRSHIPS** . . . . . . . . . . . . . . . . 40
    ANDREAS KATSINERIS-PAINE

**TO LIGHT A MATCH, TO START THE FIRE** . . 57
    BIANCA BREEN

**TIME'S KEY** . . . . . . . . . . . . . . . . . . . . . . . . . 72
    EMILY LARKIN

**SEEKING MISS KITTY** . . . . . . . . . . . . . . . . . . 93
    ADELE JONES

**THE MAP-MAKER** . . . . . . . . . . . . . . . . . . . .115
  ELIZABETH KLEIN

**DEAR SOUL CATCHER** . . . . . . . . . . . . . . .135
  ANNALIESE HUDSON

**IN A LEAGUE OF HER OWN**. . . . . . . . . . . .154
  JEANETTE O'HAGAN

**RUN** . . . . . . . . . . . . . . . . . . . . . . . . . . . . . .181
  SHAYE WARDROP

**WHAT AUNT MAUD ACHIEVED**. . . . . . . . .192
  JENNIFER HORN

**THE SPARK** . . . . . . . . . . . . . . . . . . . . . . .198
  RACHEL DENHAM-WHITE

**MEET THE AUTHORS**. . . . . . . . . . . . . . . . .223

# FOREWORD

## LYNNE STRINGER

When I edited the *Crossed Spaces* anthology in 2020, I had so much fun that when I was asked to do it again for *Stepping Sideways*, I immediately said yes.

It's always exciting to read how different authors write in certain genres and I knew that an anthology featuring either steampunk or dystopian stories would bring out some interesting and possibly dark themes. This collection certainly contains stories with immense challenges, set in worlds I'm glad I don't live in, but there are also stories of hope and rescue, of love and triumph, of overcoming evil to find a better life.

I'm proud to be involved in this anthology, both as an author and an editor. I hope that everyone who reads the stories on these pages is challenged to think a little differently as a result of reading them. But even if they don't do that, I will be happy if the stories simply entertain readers and allow them to visit another world, even if only for a sliver of time.

# EMILY LARKIN

For me, reading brings to mind the famous opening of Ray Bradbury's *Fahrenheit 451*: 'It was a pleasure to burn.' While this line refers to the destruction of books, ironically, it also reminds me of the pleasure found in reading—which, in part, is what Bradbury's book is about.

Stories can set our minds alight and our hearts aflame. Reading the right story at the right time can stoke our courage; fuel our passion, anger or determination; compel us to think, feel, and act. And, yes, to burn is so often a pleasure.

It is my hope that you find a story in this collection to set you on fire. While steampunk stories often explore alternative societies influenced by Victorian-era classes and styles, and mechanical technology that blends the old with the new, dystopian narratives explore grim societies with a glimmer of hope and rebellion stirring in the shadows—or moving into the open. The stories in this anthology span different places, time periods, and cultures; chronicle rivalries, friendships, and discoveries; fuse magic with technology; and showcase characters who confront the darkness within and without. I've long wondered why many of us are so fascinated by the otherworldly, or by tales of pasts, presents and futures that don't exist—and I think the answer is that these stories really examine human nature and the now. They offer a portal to better understand ourselves, by taking an imaginative leap or two.

To read is a pleasure, and to edit is as well. In editing this anthology with Lynne Stringer, I have been privileged to explore the terrains of other authors' imaginations. Now that the book is complete, we're delighted to invite you on a journey, to step sideways, into the alternative spaces of these narratives. Reading is the match you hold to your soul, and we hope that you burn.

# BIG TOP BREAKOUT

## LYNNE STRINGER

*You can do this. Don't give up!*

I could see Helen shaking from where I stood, by the back door of the big top. I doubted any of the towners would notice, especially since her clown makeup made her smile as wide as it could be.

Sure enough, they laughed and clapped as she dodged the custard pies CeeBee cannoned at her. He jumped up and down like a demented jack-in-a-box. It was part of the act, but the maniacal gleam in his eyes was not.

Several of the pies connected with a *splat*, slapping into Helen's back and side. She gave an exaggerated frown but was careful not to touch the pie filling.

She headed toward the exit as the act drew to a close, pies hitting her all the way. One slapped her on the butt just as she reached me. Though her eyes snapped wide, she kept up the act, putting her hands on her rear and turning back to the house. Then she gave the towners a wave and slipped out of their view.

I grabbed her hands. 'It's all right. You made it through.'

'What does he put in those things? It burns!'

I'd brought a bucketful of water with me and helped her wash the pie filling off. Some of her costume had been eaten away by it and the skin underneath was blistering.

'Out of the way, you two,' said Freda as she marched past with the liberty horses. We leapt to the side; the horses were known to take bites out of anyone who came too close. Freda preened herself a little. I knew she was hoping to catch someone's eye, someone who worked in Office or Government. They would be her ticket out of this cesspit.

I pushed aside the big top curtain and helped Helen hobble into the backyard—a tented area out of sight of the towners. My nose twitched at the odour of horse manure, musty hay and stale popcorn. I led her through the small ring where the acrobats and jugglers were practising and past the cages where the monkeys shrieked and hollered, their spittle coating the bars. Our single lion paced menacingly in his pen, letting out a rumble as we passed.

CeeBee walked past us, pushing his pie cannon. He wagged a finger at Helen. 'You weren't hit enough times, Helen, my dear.' He glared at me. 'Eva, what are you doing here? Your act is done.'

'Sorry, boss,' I said. 'We'll go back to clown alley and get changed.'

Clown alley was only a tent flap away. Each of the circus's acts had its own 'alley' where our props and costumes were kept. CeeBee wheeled his cannon into a corner, holding back the flap with a mocking bow as Helen limped in. Then, with a final sneer, he disappeared.

The cannon sat in a corner, the scent of smoke wafting from it. Maybe I could get a chisel from a prop man or even a sledgehammer from our blacksmith and smash it into the ground. But the Director came down hard on the destruction of circus property and I knew it wouldn't stop CeeBee.

We tromped over the canvas floor, mud finding its way through the holes, even though straw had been used to plug the gaps. I helped Helen into a chair in front of one of the dressing tables, where I found some salve in a drawer and applied it to her burns.

I looked at the despair on her face, which was clear even though half of the bulbs surrounding the table's mirror were blown out. The others winked sporadically, their fitful light making her look like a wraith. She drew deep breaths, tears running tracks down the white makeup caked on her face.

With a final squeeze of her shoulder, I wandered over to where Jonas was tinkering with the clown car. By some miracle, it had worked during his act. It had sat up on its rear bumper, flipped over and made a full circuit around the ring on its side with five of us inside. But he usually only tinkered when there was something wrong.

I peeked under the hood with him, but I didn't know enough about normal vehicles to have any hope of identifying the problem in a car like this. 'What's up?'

He'd already taken his makeup off, so the severity of his face peered back at me with no smile to mask it. His brown eyes were troubled as he tried to wrest something into place, his dark curls bouncing around his forehead. 'Nothing really.'

Then why the downcast look?

He glanced at Helen. Of course. We all slunk around like hunted animals when CeeBee wheeled out the pie cannon.

I went to Helen's side. She was removing her makeup and costume, revealing her short blonde bob. The red welts on her arms, back and abdomen stood out on her fair skin.

She looked bewildered. 'Why does he do that?'

'I don't know.' I had theories. It was a power play. We were under his control, we clowns. We lived and performed for him, and we needed to perform perfectly every time.

Jonas came over, wiping grease off his hands with a cloth. 'Are you okay?' He knelt next to Helen. She nodded but her eyes were bleak.

'She made it through,' I said.

'But we always do in the act, don't we? He wouldn't dream of going any further in front of the towners. But later …' Helen's shoulders shook. She'd made a mistake in the act the day before, which had led to this retribution. And CeeBee clearly felt it wasn't enough.

'I'm done, aren't I?' Her voice rose to a fever pitch. 'I won't be here when we're let out tomorrow.'

What could we say? Any denial would be full of comforting lies. I just held Helen while she sobbed, running my hand over her hair.

But Jonas had that look in his eye again. 'We can't let this happen, Eva. We have to get out somehow.'

Every time a clown disappeared, Jonas started pacing and plotting, determined to find a way to free us from our entertainment slavery. 'You said that when Olly disappeared.' And Kate and Blake and Nellie and Austin. 'The gate is only opened during the performances. There's no way she could get out without being seen. And she can't get over the fence at night.' So many had tried. 'Where would she go, anyway?'

'To my parents' farm.'

It wasn't the first time he'd mentioned the magical farm where he'd grown up, somewhere outside the system that our city operated in, somewhere that seemed so ludicrously unreal we were sure he'd made it up.

Jonas seemed oblivious to our disbelief. 'You know I ran away to join the Circus.'

'Poor fool you,' I said.

'Yeah, I know that now. But my parents are always looking for workers at harvest time. We could stay there.'

'How far away is it? It wouldn't take long for CeeBee to catch up to us.'

'Not if we had transport. And I've been hard at work since Olly …' He didn't want to say it any more than we wanted to think it.

*Since they killed him.*

'Hard at work on *what?*'

With a flourish, he gestured at the clown car.

I snorted. 'Like we'd get far in *that*.' Surely he wasn't … he couldn't actually be considering it?

I looked at the car. It only retained a faint splash of red and yellow paint. There were more patches of rust than anything else. And every time I got in it, I cut myself on a sharp edge of metal. 'It isn't exactly built for a long trip, is it?'

'I've made adjustments. I know it can get us there.'

'Tonight?'

The spark in his eyes died out and he dropped his gaze to his feet.

Helen's bottom lip trembled, but nothing could stop the tears from building. She gave a choking sob and ran away.

\*\*\*

I stood in the doorway of my cell, looking at the cells to the right and left. I could see Helen in her doorway, peering out forlornly. I wished I could do something to help.

I heard the slam as the cell doors began to shut. CeeBee came around to check each one as they came down. He adjusted his belt over his large belly and wiped a filthy hand under his nose. It was crooked, his face covered with lines and angles that gave no sense of symmetry. Rumour said he had started in the freak show and had paid a large price to have his features altered so he could leave it.

'Goodnight, Jonas,' he growled, giving Jonas no time to reply as his cell door thudded shut, blocking him from view.

Before he shut my door, he turned to Helen. 'Goodnight, Helen,' he sang. 'Sweet dreams.'

My door slammed shut and the tiny yellow light of my cell came on. I lowered myself into the chair at my dressing table, Helen's terror-filled face dancing behind my eyelids like a deranged acrobat. Slowly, it began to fade away and I filled my lungs, forcing myself to relax.

Although I hated being imprisoned in here by myself overnight, at least it was away from prying eyes. Away from having to perform, and not just for the towners. We were always trying our hardest, anything to avoid ending up a target.

Like Helen.

I looked at the newspaper clippings stuck to the dressing table mirror, clippings my parents had sent me, all saying how wonderful our Circus was. They'd even told me in a letter that they'd come to see me perform. They weren't allowed to make contact, of course.

It was only then that I realised what day it was. 'How about that?' I said aloud. 'It's my birthday tomorrow.' Yes, I would be seventeen. A year ago, I'd been about to join the Circus.

I could still hear my father's voice. *'I've heard that it's not as bad as the Zoo or the Parks. You should do okay there.'* But he hadn't looked hopeful.

I looked at my weary reflection. My eyes had lost all their spark and my skin was blotched from the constant makeup. My short brown hair was lank and sweaty from the wig I wore at every performance.

I looked around at the small basin, bed and other necessities that made up this tiny prison I was locked in every night.

Why couldn't I have been smarter, like my brother? He'd passed all his subjects with distinctions. That meant straight into a job in Government or an Office, like my dad. But I'd got my mother's brains, although at least she'd managed to get into Retail. Then her luck had continued, as Dad had spotted her, pulled her out of Retail, and married her. Now she lived in comfort and security.

People who worked in Government were the top of the chain. They had the best of everything. Not like someone in the Circus. When you were in a profession this low, the only hope of getting out was marrying someone higher, but while a man might look twice at someone like Freda in her tutu, no one would give a clown a second glance.

My father had known it too—I'd seen it in his eyes as he'd waved goodbye.

But what if Jonas was right? What if there was a world beyond here, somewhere we could be free? I had known him a year and he'd never lied to me.

It was hard to believe, but there had to be a way out of this rat-infested performance prison.

\*\*\*

The door lifted in the morning and sunlight streamed in.

I knew I shouldn't look, but I couldn't stop myself. Sure enough, Helen's cell door was wide open. Her belongings were strewn all over the floor, the dressing table broken, the mirror splintered.

Jonas walked past and I left my cell to join him. CeeBee was there, as was Hostler. Hostler's large back was hunched, his face grim. I could see despair and fury in his eyes.

CeeBee saw us and put on his usual outrage. 'Helen's run away. Can you believe it? Of all the useless, ungrateful … Look at the mess she left!'

We kept walking. We'd heard it all before.

'Escaped,' Jonas said under his breath. 'Yeah, sure.' If anyone had a hope of doing that, we'd have all been out after the first week. We never knew what happened to the ones who vanished, but they seemed to disappear from clown alley more than anywhere else in this show.

Did that mean something?

'What if I talk to the Director about this?'

Jonas's eyes nearly fell out of his head. 'Are you insane? Do you want to put a target on your back?'

It was a risk, but … 'Maybe I can do it without CeeBee knowing.'

'You know you can't.'

I didn't care what Jonas said. 'Come on, how many people go missing from acrobatics or the horses? How about the elephant team? Even the kid workers don't disappear as regularly as us.'

Jonas's nod conceded my point. 'I still don't think it's worth the risk. If CeeBee finds out …'

But I knew I couldn't just stand by and let another clown disappear.

***

CeeBee was nowhere to be found that morning. It felt like the perfect time to approach the Director.

Jonas's doubts were ringing in my ears as I went to the Director's tent. I'd only been in there once and it had been enough to tell me how different our lives were. We lived in tiny cells and were locked in at night, but the Director, the top rung of the ladder here, had his own palatial tent with several rooms. Its door flapped in the breeze as I approached, like it was waving me away.

Maybe I should have listened.

Two Security Bosses stood on either side of the door, their scowls hitting me before I'd even come close to them.

'I'm here to see the Director.' My voice was so tiny it was a wonder they could hear me.

It looked like they weren't going to let me in, but I puffed my chest out. 'We're allowed to see the Director if we need to.' It was true, but also rare. The only reason I was there was that I was more afraid of CeeBee.

One of them raised the flap and I slipped inside.

I moved into the reception area and approached the office. But my feet forced me to a standstill when I heard the voices within.

'It wasn't my fault, sir, honestly!' It was CeeBee, his words dripping with fear.

'Really, Clown Boss?' came the Director's silvery tone. 'You let that little girl push you around, didn't you?'

'But she's gone now.'

'Yes, only because *we* saw to it. Your act is the least productive here and I've seen with my own eyes how little control you have over the clowns. I suggest you show more leadership in future, or we may have to review *your* position here.'

'Yes, sir. Of course, sir.'

The same moment I realised that the Director wasn't going to help me, CeeBee, still bowing obsequiously, lifted the flap and came into the reception area.

His eyes fell on me. I could feel the guilt and fear imprinted on my face, screaming louder than any words, telling him exactly what I was doing there. His expression morphed from panic to fury. He pointed at the door.

I turned and ran, the target already on my back, just like Jonas had said. I bolted across the backyard toward clown alley, burying myself amongst the costumes.

I heard the thud of CeeBee's footfalls as he stalked by

my hiding place. Then I felt a crash of terror as he roared, 'All clowns, get in here!'

It was hard to make myself move, but it would make no difference whether I stayed cowering or went to hear the pronouncement of my fate. I crept out, trying to keep behind everyone else, their wary looks telling me they knew what to expect.

CeeBee strode up and down. 'Our performances for the past week have been woeful and Helen has defected, fled the security we offered her.' He stabbed a finger at each one of us in turn. 'You all need to do better. Jonas!'

Jonas straightened his spine as though he'd been electrocuted. 'Yes, sir?'

'That clown car needs to be funnier. You need to have more accidents. From now on, the clown car will close our set. And how many people have we had in there at most?'

'Ten, sir,' Jonas squeaked.

'Ten! That's ridiculous. I've heard of as many as forty! We have fourteen clowns here. I want *all* of them in that car at tomorrow's performance.'

I could see Jonas counting in his head as he looked around. 'There are fifteen of us.'

CeeBee's eyes shifted to me. 'I'm not counting Eva. She will be performing the custard pie routine with me tomorrow.'

All heads turned to me. I knew my face was ashen, but I also knew pleading would be useless. CeeBee always followed through. The next time I performed, I would take so many hits I could hardly walk and would disappear overnight. CeeBee's eyes glinted. He turned and stalked out of the alley.

Jonas came straight over and took hold of me. 'Eva, you

can't do it. You need to get away tonight.'

But his words were like a buzzing sound in my ears. 'You know that won't work. We've been over this.'

'We can. All of us need to go.'

I couldn't take any more of his crazy plotting. 'The car would never make it!'

'Yes it will. I told you I've been working on it. I'll make sure I finish it before the show. It *will* make it.'

He looked so certain, so steadfast. But … 'How do we get through the fence?'

'If the gate is open when we're on, we can get out.'

'The gate is only opened to let the towners in!'

His eyes searched mine, his gaze settling me enough that I could hear him. 'Do you remember who mans the gate now?'

'Hostler.' He'd been with the Circus the longest, which was one of the reasons he was entrusted with working the gate. And I'd seen myself how unhappy he'd been about Helen.

'You know he likes you,' said Jonas.

He'd been saying that for months. 'Hostler rarely says more than two words to me.'

'That's more than I've ever gotten from him. If he knows your life is on the line, he might just happen to leave the gate open. And we drive out in the clown car and head straight to my parents' farm.'

I groaned. 'It's more likely Hostler will turn me in.'

'How would that be worse? You're going to vanish anyway.'

He had a point. 'What about the other clowns?' I asked.

'They'll already be in the car. I don't think they'll object if we get them outside the fence. After that, what they do is up to them.'

So, the only problem was getting out. I shook off Jonas's arms and marched out of the alley.

***

Hostler.

The man was a mystery. He had a cell, but I'd never seen him in it. He always seemed to be on duty. Rumour had it that his parents had dumped him here when he was eight and he was way older than any of the other prop men, possibly even thirty. I didn't know how he'd survived so long.

He leant against the fence, playing with a lariat, his large frame hunched. His hair stuck out from under his hat like straw. He was chewing on some node grass, but when he saw me, he spat it out.

'Eva.' When I didn't reply, his shoulders folded back up and he resumed his game.

I wasn't convinced Hostler would help. I also knew that if he did help, he could be the next to vanish.

'Sad that Helen left,' I said.

I could see him dissecting my expression. 'Very sad.'

'I'll be doing the custard pie routine with CeeBee tomorrow.' I couldn't look at him as I said it. He wasn't a fool. He would know what that meant. I could almost feel the fog of death creep between us, a mist that would encompass me soon enough.

Did he care? He was silent so long I wasn't sure. Then I heard him gulp. 'I think you'll do well.' His tone disagreed.

My mouth was so dry it was hard to keep talking. 'The boys will be doing the clown car just afterwards. Jonas is going to make some special modifications, you know, so it can go further. I mean, do more.' Would he understand?

I was finally able to meet his eyes. Concern swam in their depths, but I could see calculation there as well. 'Hmph. Hopefully, he'll make it work.'

*Does that mean he understands?*

'You know,' he said, playing with the lariat again, 'those elephants have been so much trouble lately. I told the Director I need to get them in earlier.'

That's right. While the elephants had originally been housed within the fence, it wasn't elephant-proof. They'd charged straight through it one day and half the troupe had fled with them.

He wasn't looking at me, but I could feel electricity in the air, almost as if his calculations were making their way into my head. 'I'm surprised he let you.'

He shrugged. 'If he wants them to perform …'

'How much earlier?'

I met his eyes and there was a smile of kinship in them. 'It's at my discretion.'

'How inconvenient for you.' I didn't break from his gaze.

'Yeah, well,' he said. 'Hope the show goes well tomorrow. I'm sure you'll throw a few surprises in for the towners.'

I grinned. 'Yeah, I will. Good luck with the elephants.'

I was *nearly* sure that he was on side with the plan. But maybe it was a trap. Whatever the case, what else could I do?

\*\*\*

I took a deep breath as I waited at the entrance for my cue.

CeeBee's manic grin was undiluted by the clown makeup. 'Make sure you give them a good show.'

I let him go out first, checking my makeup in the mirror beside me. My red smile was painted wide, the red bulbous nose protruding just above it. I pulled my blond curly wig straight as I waited for Announcer to say his piece, but the previous act was still going. I had a few minutes.

No matter how hard it was, I had to at least make it through the routine. It didn't matter if I got hurt; it only mattered that I got in the car.

I heard a *chug-chug-chug* and turned to see it pulling up beside me. Jonas hopped out.

'Where are the others?' I asked.

'Still getting ready. I'll try and get as many in as I can just before CeeBee finishes and then we'll head straight for you. Hop in and we'll get out of here.'

I tried to let his faith inhabit me. Could I really believe? The car didn't look like it could do one round of the ring, much less drive us miles to a remote utopia.

It didn't matter. One way or another, this would be my last day in the Circus.

'And now,' Announcer said, his scripted words making fear clog my throat, 'be prepared to laugh until you fall into the aisles as you watch Clem and Cathy and the Custard Pie Caper!'

I watched CeeBee creep out from the flap leading to the ring, his every movement showing exaggerated evil. At least, to the towners it would look exaggerated. To me, it looked completely normal.

I picked up a ring and skipped in it, stepping out in front

of the crowd. I stumbled a few times, eyes wide, scolding the ring that had tripped me up, and the house laughed. I kept my eyes away from CeeBee as I was supposed to, ignoring it as he pantomimed shooting the cannon at me, so it seemed that I was the only one unaware of what he was doing.

The opposite was true, of course. The towners had no idea CeeBee's shots had a reputation for being lethal.

My heart was hammering as I watched him line up the cannon while I continued my business with the ring. Then, just as he was ready to fire, I turned, as if seeing him for the first time. I made my face horror-struck (not that difficult), then started to run before tripping over the ring again.

*Bang!* CeeBee's first shot grazed my shoulder, knocking me to the side. I managed to salvage the fall, making it look like part of the routine, even though my collarbone felt like it was on fire. I ignored it and jumped to my feet, continuing to pantomime terror to the house.

It was a good thing they didn't know it was real.

*Bang!* The next shot glanced my ribs, knocking the breath out of me. It was difficult to save the fall and get up again. There were scorch marks on my costume.

Three rapid shots later, I was grateful only one had scored a direct hit, sweeping out my leg. I nearly screamed in agony but dragged myself to my feet.

Should I run?

I heard the *aawoohah* of the car horn as it shot into view, bringing a scowl to CeeBee's face. It did a circuit of the ring, Jonas standing it on its rear, then leaning it on the side, clown arms and legs sticking out in all directions.

The car was full. We were taking *everyone?* How the hell was I supposed to get in?

Jonas pulled up beside me. 'Quick, Eva. The roof!'

The roof of the car was fitted with handles, which we used for tricks. I leapt on top, grabbing them, as Jonas sped toward the exit and CeeBee lined up his final shot. It caught the rear of the car and it skidded, jarring my hands as they smashed against the handholds. I grit my teeth, ignoring the pain, and kept my place, even as my legs careened out over the side and my stomach rammed into the roof.

Was the car going to roll? It was designed to, but Jonas kept it steady, heading straight through clown alley and out into the backyard.

I knew that CeeBee would have to make it look like part of the show. He wouldn't be able to race out after us, screaming and promising swift retribution.

But there ahead of us was that insurmountable obstacle—the fence. Two metres high chain link that caged in the whole circus. Barbed wire at the top. They'd added that after a few had managed to throw themselves over and scamper off.

And the gate was shut.

I was about to scream at Jonas to stop—that we'd failed—when I saw the elephants lumbering along with their keepers. They weren't close enough for Hostler to open the gate yet and he seemed oblivious to our presence.

Jonas didn't stop.

Although the elephants were still too far away, Hostler casually swung the gate open, then looked around, mouth hanging open, as we drove past him to freedom. I looked back and saw him scratch his head and frown.

I didn't know he could act. He wasn't bad.

We raced down the street, through the township, all the way to its outskirts and up a hill, driving until we hit the beginning of a forest trail. Then Jonas braked and I nearly somersaulted onto the bonnet of the car, the bones in my hands creaking. I was stiff from hanging on to the roof and flexed my fingers as he jumped out and helped me off.

Out piled thirteen more clowns! We'd broken the car record.

But there was no time for congratulations. 'We've got to keep going,' I said.

Jonas turned to the others. 'We're heading for my parents' farm. It's a bit of a hike from here, but I know they'll help us. You're welcome to come if you like or you can go your own way.'

Eight of them had disappeared into the forest before he'd finished speaking. Five others paused to shake hands before they too, left us.

In the end, there was only Jonas and me left.

Through the trees fringing the forest, I could see the lights of the circus. Too far away to see the smoke rising from Cook's firepit or smell the roasting meat and elephant dung. Now there was only the scent of pine and grass.

No more circus. No more threats. No more fear. No more slavery.

I turned to Jonas. 'Please tell me your stories were true. Your parents are real? They'll take me in?'

He took my hands, caressing the bruises that were already forming. 'I'm sure of it. They're always looking for help, especially at this time of year. Even if they weren't, they won't turn us away.

After all,' he gestured at his costume, 'we're dressed to entertain.'

'All right then,' I said. 'We'd better get going before CeeBee catches up to us.'

We got back into the car, which seemed incredibly spacious now that there were only two of us.

'Let's go, Jonas.' I smiled at him.

'Told you it would work.' He gave me a triumphant grin.

Fair enough. After all, his crazy plan had been the key to our big top breakout.

# MECHANICAL MAGIC

## LINSEY PAINTER

Freedom was within her grasp. All Nix had to do was take two steps, jump through the doorway of the engine's cab, leap far enough to clear the bridge and plunge into the Thames. She could smell the briny tang in the air and just catch the cries of seagulls above the locomotive's piercing whistle. She could imagine the cool waters welcoming her home.

Nix took a step, then froze. If she went back now, she'd never know what life was like on land. Yet almost as soon as she'd placed her unsteady feet on firm ground, she'd been press-ganged into working on Lord Scrumpton's steam engine.

*Confound it!* This infernal conflict was tossing her about like a wave on the sea.

Being human was supposed to be exciting and adventurous. Instead, she'd spent the last three weeks covered in soot and scuttling around after orders like a crab.

Big Ben's immense tower and clockface rose in the distance, snagging her attention. The majestic spires of yellow brick and myriad glass windows that glinted in the sun were unlike any of the coral structures she'd grown up with.

An ear-splitting whistle and jarring rattle pulled Nix out of her reverie. The bridge had ended.

*Blast!* She'd missed her chance at freedom.

She swayed with the floor's rumble and rocking. She touched her chest and felt the soft, magic red cap she kept hidden beneath her strapped breasts. As long as she had her skull cap she could transform back into her merrow form at any time. She was a maiden of the sea and she was here on *her* terms.

'Stoker!' The voice of Driver hit her like a slap.

Nix snapped to attention.

'Stop yer dreamin' and see to the fire,' he growled.

Nix glared at the man through her smudged goggles. *Slave driver.* She grunted as she shovelled another load of coal. After three weeks she still felt the weight of being human. Every movement was heavy and laborious like she had hard coral wrapped around her body.

'You might think you're onto a good thing when 'is Lordship treats you better'n the rest of us,' Driver barked. 'But them that's in high places can't always be trusted. 'Specially ones who don't have no bees and honey.' He pulled a lever and a cloud of steam obscured the view outside before dissipating.

Nix scratched the back of her shorn head. 'I don't understand.'

'His Lordship don't got no money.'

Nix squinted at Driver through her goggles. Humans were so strange. Lord Scrumpton was … well … a lord. This was his train. Aristocracy were, in her experience, very wealthy. 'Lord Scrumpton is a gentleman.'

Driver harumphed. 'He looks a right dandy; a desperate one. Desperate means dangerous.'

Nix gazed around the cab taking in the burnished cogs and patched-up flooring.

'You just watch yerself, lad. Scrumpton'd sell his soul to the highest bidder if it meant getting his hands on cash. He wouldn't think twice about selling you.'

A dark blur flashed past Nix's face. She flinched away then cried out as a small bundle of smoky black feathers fell onto the coal pile. Driver grunted and pushed past Nix. He knelt and stared intently at the tiny bird.

'Is it dead?' Nix said in a whisper.

'Just stunned,' Driver said, his usually gruff voice hushed. 'Leave it be. It'll come 'round.'

Before she could reply, a familiar clink and squeak sounded in the gangway. Nix raised her head. Only one person made so much noise when walking. Lord Scrumpton's mechanical leg could be heard above the rhythmic clank of the train, the hiss of steam and even the shrill whistle that sounded at every crossing and station.

Lord Scrumpton's hulking form filled the doorway. He towered over Nix. From his black satin top hat to his massive brass-buckled boots, monocle and mutton chops, Lord Scrumpton was truly a sight to behold. Some said his heart was as hard and rusty as his prosthesis, but so far, the man had treated her with a rough kindness. It seemed to amuse him that she was educated.

'Nix, my boy, how are you?' His voice boomed.

'Well, sir,' Nix said.

'That's the ticket,' he replied. 'Come, take a turn about this mechanical beast with me. Curly will take your duties for a bit.' He didn't wait for an answer but turned and walked away, expertly moving with the train's sway, coat tails flapping.

Nix hurried after him, pushing her shovel into Curly's small hands. Poor Curly—he was bottom feeder since she'd moved up to stoker.

The train went through a tunnel and Nix saw her reflection in the windows. What a sight she was. Her mother wouldn't recognise her. Her green hair was shorn. Sooty oversized overalls, newsboy cap and neck kerchief completed her disguise. At her mother's insistence, Nix had masqueraded as a boy when she'd surfaced for her venture on land. She shuddered now to think what might have been her fate if her captors found out she was female. Only her eyes—the colour of a stormy grey-green sea—were still recognisable, though they were bloodshot from smoke and twelve-hour shifts.

The clink and squeak—and occasional pause as the rusty prosthesis seized up—accompanied them through the carriages. They passed through the musty, dusty postage and baggage cars. After what Driver had revealed about Lord Scrumpton's financial state, the worn out, unkempt state of the train was now obvious.

'This infernal leg is driving me mad,' Lord Scrumpton growled as he tapped it sharply with his cane. They lumbered by passengers in seating compartments, the upholstery and carpets worn and faded.

'Perhaps, Your Lordship, you are in need of a replacement.'

Scrumpton chuckled. 'I've got a mechanical wizard on board today. Or maybe she's a witch. They say she can repair any contraption that is broken and create mechanical masterpieces beyond your wildest dreams.'

They attempted to tiptoe through the dimly lit sleeper carriage—its silence punctuated with occasional snores—and entered the disused lounge car.

'Her creations are so lifelike that you'd think the machines could actually breathe.' Scrumpton stopped suddenly and Nix almost ran into the back of him. 'But do you think I could get this *wizard* to give my prosthesis a look over?' He frowned deeply. 'No. It costs an arm and a leg to fix a stiff, noisy prosthesis. And there's no ready money.' He tapped his leg again. 'I could be walking smooth and silent as a lion stalking its prey. Instead, I make enough noise to wake the dead.'

Heads turned as they continued, passing through the hot, steamy kitchen car.

'Engines are the future,' Scrumpton rhapsodised loudly, over the bang and clash of pots and pans. 'If we can just harness their full potential there's no end to what can be done.'

'Perhaps sir, you need to find something this … *wizard* desires,' Nix offered.

'Indeed,' said Scrumpton, tapping his cane to the side of his head. He glanced at her, narrowing his eyes. 'I think you might be onto something.'

The rich smell of sweet, buttery cakes wafted through the carriage. Nix's stomach growled. Human food was one of the most tantalising of torments. So many tempting smells drifted from the kitchen car but all she'd tasted so far was stodgy, bland gruel.

'A bit hungry, are you, lad?'

Nix nodded eagerly.

'That's the ticket,' Scrumpton said with a chuckle. 'A growing boy like you needs more than slave's skilly.'

Nix's heart leapt at the thought of her stomach being full for once, and to finally experience exotic flavours swimming across her tongue.

Scrumpton studied her with a critical eye. 'Wash up first though, lad. Won't do to get soot on the ladies.' He clapped his hand. 'Shake a leg!'

Minutes later, they entered the busy dining car. Nix caught sight of one of the patrons inside and anger surged through her like lava in a volcano.

'It's little Nixie,' boomed a familiar, unwelcome voice. Nix tried to tamp down on the gathering eruption as she moved forward. 'Tell us how the stoking business goes.'

Raucous laughter followed and Nix stumbled as Squid Stevens slapped her hard across the back of her shoulders. His loud cannon laugh burst out and shook the hanging gas lamps.

Nix glared up at the lanky sailor who stood beside her, a smirk on his face. Squid had been one of her original captors and enjoyed reminding her of it. She forced her gaze away. *Slimy rapscallion.*

An unfamiliar lady, tall and fashionably dressed, stood behind one chair. She wore a deep purple fitted tunic embroidered with gold symbols of clockwork. A tiny satin hat perched atop a pile of chestnut curls.

Nix studied the lady's beautiful clothes with longing. In contrast, Nix looked like an unwashed street urchin, and a boy at that.

'Miss Foxy Brown,' Lord Scrumpton crooned, kissing the lace-gloved hand the lady held out. He pulled out a chair for her and she gracefully sat. 'Allow me to introduce Master Nix, a first-rate stoker and conversationalist.'

Nix bowed at the waist.

'A pleasure, I am sure,' the lady said. Her dark eyes studied Nix from behind a short veil.

'You'll have to forgive the appearance of our stoker,' Squid Steven's voice filled the carriage. 'He's had a hard week. Slavery isn't for the faint-hearted.'

Nix smiled tightly. Another loud guffaw blasted from Squid. Anticipating his next move, Nix neatly sidestepped his second slap and stuck her foot out. His momentum set him off balance. Staggering, he tripped over Nix's foot and sprawled across the table. Those seated leapt up as coffee and cakes spilled into laps and hot liquid splashed on expensive clothing. Lord Scrumpton roared in pain.

Nix raced for the nearest exit as Squid let out an almighty bellow. What had she done? Dashing through the door, she burst into a narrow corridor. Passengers flattened themselves against the wall. Nix barrelled through them, their angry shouts pursuing her in her desperate escape.

A door crashed behind her. She glanced back to see Squid leap through the exit she'd taken.

Her thoughts darted about in a frenzy. What would she do once she'd reached the end of the train? She was trapped like a seal in a net. She didn't want to contemplate what the weedy fisherman would do if he caught her.

As the train careened around a corner, she slammed into the door of the last carriage. Her lungs aching, she jerked it open and stumbled haphazardly down the aisle between the open seats and gaping passengers. She wrenched open the final door which led to the observation balcony and gasped. Another carriage? They'd hooked it up at the last station. It had completely slipped her mind.

Frosty wind whipped past her. She clung to the fencing rail of the balcony as the train raced around another curve, shuddering and swaying. Could she get across? There was no undercover gangway, just a coupling linking the strange carriage to the rest of the train.

Squid hollered behind her and Nix scrambled up onto the slippery rails. A roar of rage sounded again, and then a crash.

She leapt, soaring over the gap and tumbling into a heap on the other side. She lay stunned for a moment, then shakily stood. Nix pushed the door open, slumped inside and locked the door behind her. Breathless, she scanned for a place to hide. But at the sight before her, Nix's eyes widened.

The carriage was an enormous room steeped in luxury. Elegant windows glinted under the glow of glass candle globes. Intricately woven oriental rugs dressed the polished wood floors and a huge silk-canopied bed filled one end.

Nix scratched her head. The opulence of the carriage was in stark contrast to the tired, rundown train. Perhaps it belonged to Miss Foxy Brown?

A floor-to-ceiling book-lined shelf took up the majority of one wall. A long workbench hugged the opposite wall and accommodated an assortment of tools, glass boxes and domes.

Nix moved towards the bench, her astonishment growing with each step.

A gush of birdsong filled the room. She jumped, her heart dancing wildly like a fish on a hook. Next to the workbench, a bird was perched on an ornate stand. Nix turned to examine it.

A liquid warble spilt from its open beak. The bird's emerald and gold feathers glimmered under the lights. The song died, its bronze beak snapped shut, and the bird bowed its head and was still. Although life-like, its stance was stiff and feathers unnatural in their colouring. It was a machine.

Nix glanced around in wonder. Her eyes landed on a group of butterflies, gently fluttering brilliant titian and turquoise wings inside a glass dome. She peered closer. They weren't butterflies, they were fairies. Their metallic skin caught the light, tiny gears spun slowly in their transparent chests, and vacant glass eyes stared beyond her. She shivered. Clockwork fairies!

What was this place? Nix's stomach began to churn. There was something strangely life-like in the creatures. They were machines and yet …

With mounting trepidation, she moved along the bench to a small stack of books. Round spectacles lay on top of a volume left open. Nix's breath caught in her throat as she spied the illustration. It was a perfect etching of a merrow—complete with a glimmering red cap hugging her head of seaweed green hair.

The air in the room felt heavy and hot. Nix pulled out her own red cap from its hiding place beneath her shirt. Like a skull cap, it was smaller and more pliable than her bulky newsboy cap and shimmered under the gas lamps. No matter how covered in soot and sweat she was, the cap remained pristine.

'Hasn't anyone told you that curiosity leads to trouble?'

Nix whirled. Foxy Brown stood in the doorway. Squid Stevens glared at Nix over Foxy's shoulder. Her stomach plunged.

'He's been 'ere a while. Just like you wanted,' said Squid.

'Perfect,' Foxy said.

Nix retreated further into the room. What did she mean?

'You may go.' Foxy dismissed Squid with a flick of her wrist.

'I-I am sorry,' Nix stammered. 'I did not mean to snoop. I was just trying to get away from …' She gestured at Squid's retreating back. The red cap in her hand flashed like a signal fire. She whisked it behind her back.

Foxy narrowed her eyes and Nix's heart froze. Why had she exposed her cap?

'What do you think of my creations?' Foxy said airily, closing the carriage door.

Relief washed over her like a wave. Maybe Foxy hadn't noticed anything unusual. 'I've never seen anything like them.'

'Improvements on the original, don't you agree?'

Nix shrugged, unable to shake the queasy feeling in the pit of her stomach as she recalled the fairies' vacant stare.

Foxy headed for the bird. 'Song thrushes have a beautiful call but are quite plain, really. Why give a little brown bird such a melodious voice?'

Foxy put her finger out and the tiny bird hopped onto it. The thrush opened its beak to let out a song but Foxy snapped it shut. 'Though it does grow tiresome with repetition.' She moved on. 'Do you like my fairyflies? Brilliant, aren't they? They understand English, of course, but they are wild and unpredictable.'

Nix's stomach clenched as she gazed at the fairyflies. They seemed lethargic compared to the grace and fluidity of real butterflies. 'What's wrong with them?'

'I drugged them,' Foxy said, with a careless shrug. 'They are a bit wilful. Always wanting to escape.'

'Wilful? Are they not machines?' Nix said, squinting to get a better look through the glass dome. 'Can you not simply turn them off?'

'My machines are the best parts of the natural,' Foxy said, 'perfected by my additions.' She waved a lace-gloved hand over her workbench.

Nix shuddered. 'Are they alive?'

'In a manner of speaking, yes.' Foxy's eyes lit. 'I could hardly be so proud of purely mechanical creations.' She tapped her chin. 'The fairies, of course, had their own magic to begin with. They have been my most successful transformation so far. It's always helpful to have a touch of magic in the metamorphosis.'

'But how?'

'I'm planning to exhibit them at the Crystal Palace,' Foxy interrupted. 'Though the queen would probably like to see something more exotic than a finagle of unruly fairies. Don't you think?'

Nix's heart fisted at the lady's appraising gaze.

'I've been working on something that I think someone of your obvious class and education would appreciate.' Foxy motioned Nix over to a box she hadn't seen earlier. 'Mythical sea creatures are a particular obsession of mine.'

Nix placed her hand over her mouth at the scene that greeted her. A miniature seal basked on a rock. A moment later, its skin split open and the head and shoulders of a woman emerged. Like a clockwork toy winding down, her movements slowed to a halt; then rewinding, she disappeared inside her mottled seal skin only to re-emerge, repeating her actions.

'She's stuck,' Foxy said in disgust. 'She was to be my

magnum opus but I cannot get her to emerge fully. Unless I solve this conundrum all she's good for is the dustbin. My creations are to be magical, not malfunctional.'

Nix stared at Foxy in horror. 'But what about who she is?'

'What about it?'

Bile rose in Nix's throat.

'That's an intriguing red cap you have there, boy.'

With growing dread, Nix followed the lady's gaze to her hand. Her red cap peeked out from her fist like an expensive silk headpiece.

The lady smirked. 'Are you thieving from the good folk on this train?'

Indignation rose hot in Nix's chest. 'I do not steal. It was my ... my mother's,' she fumbled.

There was a rapid *rat-a-tat-tat* on the door and Foxy glided across the room, brushing past Nix on her way. Nix frantically tried to quell the panic that threatened to break out of her like a tidal wave. She wiped her sweaty hands down her overalls.

Driver stood outside. 'Pardon, madam. Lord Scrumpton has sent me to fetch the stoker.'

Foxy stepped aside and gestured for Nix to come. 'Here he is. He was helping me with some ... research.'

Nix practically leapt for the door, squeezing past Foxy's bustled skirt. She gulped in the brisk air.

'Come on, lad,' Driver said as they walked back. 'His Lordship's none too 'appy wit' t' likes of you.' They crossed from Foxy's carriage to the rest of the train, a sturdy ramp making the crossing much less adventurous. 'Best you stay up front with me, lad. That lady's nothing but trouble.'

\*\*\*

Scoop, turn, step, toss, step, turn, scoop. Her actions repeated again and again; mechanical motion like a cog on a wheel, like pistons pumping and pushing, like wheels racing with a clackety-clack—the syncopated rhythm of the train on the track. After six hours of scooping and shovelling, she'd become part of the engine.

Nix clenched her hands and stopped. The train kept going, every part moving except for her.

She could choose. And what she wanted now was to be home.

The small box under Driver's seat drew her attention. The tiny swift, now recovered, regarded her with bright eyes. It probably wanted to go home too.

Nix slumped against her shovel. The heat sapped her of strength and dried up every drop of water from her parched mouth and dehydrated body.

'What are you doin', Stoker?' growled Driver. 'Back to work, lad.'

'I need water,' she rasped. Her tongue felt twice its normal size and dry as a desert.

'You just had water.'

'That was two hours ago.'

'What are you, a fish?' Driver thrust a jar of water at her.

Nix gulped down the water, coughing and spluttering when she inhaled it in her haste.

'Back to work,' Driver growled. 'If we don't keep this train movin', we'll be payin' with our rations.'

Nix touched her chest, wanting to feel the comfort of her red cap strapped underneath her clothes … but there was nothing there.

She almost howled in alarm. She cast her eyes around the engine room but there was nothing on the floor.

'What's the matter with you now, lad?' Driver's voice grated.

She searched her mind for the last time she'd had it. Foxy's carriage! Had she dropped it or had Foxy stolen her cap right out of her hand?

'Buck up, boy. We'll be crossin' the North Channel tonight on that brand new bridge,' Driver said, wiping his brow. 'You always perk up when we get in sight of water. We'll reach the coast of Scotland by the gloamin'. From there, it'll take less than an hour to cross the bridge to Ireland.'

Driver reached into the box where the swift sat. 'I'll drop this wee one off tonight. It will find its way home. I can't stand to see creatures trapped.' He fixed Nix with a loaded stare. 'You'd best be going home too, lad.'

Nix wanted to cry. A perfect time to escape and she'd lost her only means.

'Nix, my boy.' Lord Scrumpton's voice boomed. Her heart jumped. Scrumpton stood next to the coal tender, a satisfied smile playing at his lips. 'Come with me.'

Nix gave her shovel to Curly. Driver placed a gloved hand on her arm. 'Remember the bridge,' he said in a low whisper, then turned his back. Nix followed Scrumpton, her heart pounding in time with the train wheels. Faster, faster, faster. Amid the clank of moving wheels, the hiss of steam and a cacophony of voices as they strode through the carriages, something was missing.

Nix shot a look at Scrumpton's prosthetic leg. It wasn't making any noise. No squeaks or clinks, no seizing up. Her stomach rolled like a wave.

He opened the door to the observation balcony. Foxy Brown waited on the landing.

Scrumpton gave Nix a little push. 'You belong to the lady now. No more stoking fires for you. You're going up in the world.'

'You can't just give me away,' Nix shouted in desperation. 'I'm not a piece of your train!'

'Of course you're not, lad,' Scrumpton said, putting his heavy hand on Nix's shoulder. 'But needs must where the devil drives.' Scrumpton chuckled, tapping his refurbished mechanical leg with his cane.

'A pleasure doing business with you again,' Foxy said as they shook hands.

Scrumpton turned and left the carriage.

Nix's heart plunged to the bottom of the ocean.

\*\*\*

Foxy ushered Nix into her carriage. 'It seems you have everyone on this train bamboozled.' She flipped off her newsboy cap. 'But I've been doing some interesting research.' She circled Nix like a shark. 'A girl, and of the fin folk at that.' Foxy held up her red cap, eyes glinting. 'You dropped something in your hurry to leave.'

Nix lunged for it—her escape.

Foxy whisked it out of her reach. 'Valuable, I see.' Foxy picked up the book Nix had seen earlier. 'The merrow, from Irish folklore,' she read. 'Otherwise known as mermaids, merrow use an enchanted red cap to aid them in their transformation from deep sea to land and back again.' Foxy looked up from the book as if trying to peel back the layers of her disguise. 'Oh yes, and they have green hair.'

Panic surged through Nix.

Foxy studied the red cloth. 'I ran some tests on your little cap. There's transformation magic woven through every strand.'

Nix's heart flailed.

'How providential,' Foxy said. 'I've been looking for one of your kind.'

Nix snatched the cap from Foxy's grasp and leapt for the door. An instant later, she crashed to the floor. Pain flashed up her chest and exploded through her tongue. The metallic taste of blood filled her mouth.

Nix rolled over. 'Please, I just want to go home.'

Foxy unhooked her umbrella from Nix's foot. 'I'm sure you do. But from now on you do my bidding.' Foxy laughed and reclaimed the cap. 'You should be thanking me. I'll show you freedom like you've never had before. Freedom from the confines of being a human slave or a *restless* merrow.'

'Like your fairies?' Nix asked, her voice trembling.

'The fairies are troublesome.' Foxy tapped her chin. 'Though now their life is a trifle stifled. My fault.' Foxy shrugged. 'I allowed too much freedom.'

*Freedom?* A whimper escaped Nix's lips.

'There, there, my dear. Foxy will make everything *better*.'

\*\*\*

Nix curled her body in the darkening carriage. The ticking of the clock on the bedside stand reverberated in her head. It was almost half past six. Foxy had left more than an hour ago to take high tea in the dining car. With her went the magic. All Foxy needed to do was bind Nix's hands and tie her to the bed. Nix could not leave without her cap.

What would Foxy to do her? Would she turn her into a machine? An exotic exhibit to be put on display and perform on demand?

The train lurched to a halt, brakes squealing and whistle shrieking. Nix sprawled across the floor and Foxy's umbrella fell with a thud near her foot. Then slowly, the train began to move again, chuffing and chugging.

The carriage tilted. The train was climbing, needing to be pushed up the incline. They had come to the bridge.

Nix opened her eyes. It would take less than an hour for the train to cross the North Channel. She sat up. One hour to escape, one hour to get her cap back, one hour to take back her freedom. She wouldn't give in to fear. She hadn't when she'd emerged from the water to discover what life was like as a human. She wouldn't now. She would escape.

Nix strained against the rope that bound her wrists. She rubbed and twisted, flexed and let her hands go limp. Her wrists burned and bled, but the rope held.

Briny sea air filtered through the windows. Nix clamped her lips together and strained with all her strength. The knot tightened.

Nix slumped. Even if she escaped the bonds, she was still without her cap. A strong undertow of despair spiralled around her. She searched the dark carriage for something to aid her. All she could make out were shadows.

The clock struck seven, the chimes ringing out. She had only half an hour left, if that!

Her eyes fell on a dark, elongated object at her feet. Foxy's umbrella. She stretched her leg out. Using her feet, she slid the umbrella up to her bound hands. Holding it between her knees, she wedged the tip between the ropes. If she could just get *some* leverage!

The cold steel of the tip pressed hard into her wrists. She scrambled to her knees to use her body weight to press down. The train lurched and she fell hard on the umbrella. The tip sprang open and the ropes sliced free.

Nix let out a squeak and her drowning heart surfaced. How had that happened? A blade stuck out from the top end of the umbrella. The tip was razor sharp. Foxy was a devious one.

She rose, headed towards the workbench and lit the gas lamp. A warm glow vanquished the shadows. She removed the glass dome encasing the fairies. A heavy, sweet scent rose into the room and Nix jumped back, holding her breath. Would they come out of their lethargy in time?

Next, she set the song thrush free, breaking its chain. It fluttered around the room, pecking the silk wall hangings and scratching at the carpet.

A furious whirring and clicking filled the room. Nix turned to see the fairies swarm like angry bees. They picked up needle-sharp tools from Foxy's workbench and flew at Nix. She ducked. 'Wait,' she said. 'I'm not your enemy. I need your help!'

The key rattled in the lock outside. Nix spun to see the door swing open and Foxy standing there, her eyes wildly scanning the chaos. She had tucked Nix's red cap into her waistband like a trophy.

Before Foxy could say a word, the fairies swarmed her, buzzing around her face and pulling at her veil. The song thrush swooped at her head. The lady spun, swatting at the fairies and dodging the thrush before crashing to the floor. The fairies swooped upon her, holding her at bay with their sharp tools while Nix tied Foxy up with the rope that had held her captive moments before.

Nix snatched up her cap. The fairies took off through the open door to freedom and the thrush followed. But there was yet one more thing Nix had to do.

'You can't leave,' screamed Foxy. 'You belong to me.'

Nix raced to the box in the corner. She reached in and with utmost care, picked up the tiny selkie. She was soft and warm in her seal shape. Nix inhaled sharply as the seal wiggled in her hand. She brought her palm up level to her eyes. 'I'm going to set you free.'

The creature regarded her with dull black eyes. She enfolded the seal in her cap and tucked it inside her pocket.

She burst through the open door and slammed it shut. The key still hung in the lock. Her hands shook as she turned it. The door barely muffled Foxy's shrieking.

Nix peered over the railings as the carriage swayed and the wind tore at her clothes. In the distance, she could make out the dark shape of land, looming larger by the second. She didn't have much time. She could see the lights of the approaching town. Her heart pounded as she wrenched her gaze away and focused on the heaving dark ocean below.

She heard Foxy's shouts of rage. The bonds would not hold her for long. She climbed onto the wrought iron railing. The massive steel cables of the bridge flashed past.

A shot rang out and Nix flinched, almost losing her balance. Foxy was free. There was an almighty crash and crazed screech, then the woman stood in the doorway, pistol in hand, eyes wild. 'No!' she screamed.

Nix sprang as far as she could and plunged over the side of the bridge. Waves rose to embrace her in their foaming surge and she knifed through the frigid waters that stole her breath. Deeper and deeper she dove. Her lungs ached then burned, but still she swam on. Cold seeped into her body. Her muscles seized.

Forcing movement from her stiff hands, she withdrew her cap from her pocket and unwrapped the tiny selkie. Life flashed in its velvet eyes. It rubbed its nose on hers and wriggled its flippers. Joy flooded Nix as the selkie cavorted in front of her.

Nix pressed her cap to her head. Perhaps her time as a human hadn't been a total disaster after all.

An itch began in her feet and shot up her legs as they fused. Gills opened up under her jawline and oxygen filled her lungs. Strength coursed through her body. Light and warmth encircled her. Scales rippled up her torso.

Nix gave a powerful kick and, with the selkie, surged through the sea.

# LENA OF THE AIRSHIPS

## ANDREAS KATSINERIS-PAINE

We lived in the mists. They hung like dark sails over the ocean from dawn to bleak midday, from suffocating night to lonely dawn again. Each morning our houses were surrounded by sheets of fog, and we stumbled through stormy vapours down to our boats each day. We breathed in mist; we practically drank it when sailing. We lived in almost total blindness.

Mist rumbled against my windowpane. I sighed. Fog would be thick over the water today, and crossings were always rougher in angry mist. The vapours could buffet a man overboard, and I lived on Island Eighteen amongst the heaviest fog.

Many sailors perished from hypothermia each year too, but I would never step outside without two knitted jumpers on. I had no choice but to sail in complete darkness most days, and to steer by the feel of the currents rather than by sight. In my case the saying was true: rough waters either make a good sailor or a dead one.

I watched my reflection in the glass for a moment. Dark brown eyes stood out against pale skin and salt-white hair. I dressed warmly, and went into the kitchen where my guardian, Vanto, sat smoking a pipe. The air was already thick with the smell of burning seaweed. He pulled out a chair.

'G'day to you, on the day of your Matching.'

'Thanks, Vanto.'

'Nervous?'

'A little.'

He got up and brought me a plate of bread and a cold boiled potato. 'Well, my last task as guardian is to remind you of today's importance. It's the biggest day in a young sailor's life, the day of the Matching Ceremony.'

He drew a breath. I could tell that he was about to deliver a boring speech learned off by heart from a Guardhouse paper; even he looked uninterested.

'Every person in our society serves an immense duty,' he began. 'Baby boys are sent to the Islands to become sailors. Baby girls go to the Academies to become ladies. We have only these two roles in the world. Young sailors have male guardians to look after them as they hop about the Islands. Ladies have a female guardian who instructs them in arts that we sailors can only guess at.

'Then at age sixteen, all sailors and ladies are brought to the Guardhouse to be Matched. Sailor with lady. They produce children, who immediately enter the care of the Guardhouse, becoming sailors and ladies in their turn. The circle continues.'

He saw that I was hardly listening and rapped his hand against the arm of his chair. 'You're aware of what happens next, then?'

'Of course,' I said, munching the stale bread. 'We become guardians to the next generation. I'm sent to an Island to live out my days watching over a young sailor. My lady goes to teach at an Academy.' I had read the same Guardhouse papers.

'There's one more option,' Vanto said. 'That of Retirement. The Guardhouse may offer it to you if you'd prefer to live long hours with your lady in front of cosy fires on far-flung Islands. Many who are offered it decide to become guardians anyway, of course. Very few sacrifice their careers for comfort.'

He had finished speaking or so it seemed. I finished my breakfast and stood.

'Good luck today, young Joro,' Vanto said. 'You're one of our better sailors. No doubt you'll be matched to a fine young lady.' He shook my hand. 'Are you going straight to the Guardhouse or paying a visit to Bersho first?'

I shook my head. 'Not Bersho. I'll see him soon enough. I'm going to visit old man Poro.'

'Ah, of course. Pass on my regards. Goodbye, Joro.' With that, he turned and went to his room.

I sighed. Vanto had never been a man of deep feelings. He could never tell when somebody was happy or sad, when they needed comfort or celebration. Having him as a guardian was like being looked after by a wooden post.

I shouldn't complain. Meals came (though they were tasteless), bedding was always provided (though it was rarely clean) and he was always present for a conversation (which often turned out to be less interesting than silence).

I went outside and readied my boat. It was a life of duty we lived, I reflected as I glanced back at our ramshackle house, with very few comforts. Our role was to pass messages and food between the Islands, to keep the watery network going, and I supposed I'd never believed in Retirement because it sounded too good to be true. A pleasant rest and a warm fire every night instead of mists, freezing waters and unknown dangers …

But I shook my head. I didn't want to think about the dangers. I didn't even want to think about Retirement. I'd always spent my free hours helping my friends Bersho and Tenko to row, holding their boats steady so they didn't capsize. I felt like it was my responsibility to help others, and I'd feel guilty about Retiring.

The fog wasn't too deadly between my Island and Poro's. After some hard rowing, the winds eventually took hold of my sails and sped me onwards. I crunched down onto his Island and tied up.

Poro's house was snug. He had lit the fire at the end of the main room and was warming his hands before the toasty blaze. When I entered, he exclaimed, 'Joro, my boy! What are you doing here? Shouldn't you be at the Guardhouse?'

'I came to see you one last time, to see that you were alright.'

His smile fell. 'It was good of you to come, lad. I enjoy seeing a friendly face now I don't have Tenko around. I always thought I'd cope well enough if I happened to lose my sailor. But on a day like today, I can't help but think of the life he's never going to live.' He raised a glass before the fire. 'He was a great fellow, wasn't he? He would have made a marvellous guardian. Better sailor than most, and a wonderful friend to you.' He watched the fire awhile in silence, then he asked, 'You saw the monster that took him, didn't you?'

'From a distance.' I felt my voice tightening.

'What was it? A fish? Some kind of shark?'

'I don't really know … Some deep, dark shape came up beneath him. He grabbed his oars but didn't have time to row. A huge creature leapt from the water … closed its jaws over his boat. Spray was everywhere, I couldn't see much. Then the monster fell back into the water and he was gone.'

I didn't add that I had been dreaming of that deep, dark shape every night since, waking in sweat.

Poro turned and looked sadly out the window. His face was creased from the salt of the mists. He was thirty-five—a very old age for guardians—and he coughed. 'Tell you the truth, lad, I may be joining Tenko very soon. This damn fog. The Guardhouse says there's nothing in it, but I think it kills us all in the end—those of us who survive the monsters. Some poison left over after the War and the End Times is my guess.'

He sat and sank his head into his hands. 'I'm sorry, lad. I don't mean to bring you down on Matching Day.' His voice cracked. 'I know a guardian isn't meant to love the sailor they look after. We're only meant to bring them up right and then pass them on to the Matching. But Tenko was special to me. I cared about him, I admired him. There used to be a word for a guardian who felt a true connection to his sailor—a *father*.' He dried a tear from his eye. 'On a day like today, I feel very much like a father.'

He stood suddenly and rubbed his hands together. 'Anyways, I've been meaning to give you something. It's a piece of machinery Tenko found on an Island in the south a few days before he was taken, from some old vessel from before the End Times. Too heavy to bring the whole thing back, but he brought one piece. Perhaps it can be of some use to the authorities at the Guardhouse.'

Poro left the room and returned lugging a large hunk of metal. It was rusty and a shape I'd never seen before, with two long blades fixed on a central hub. He carried it out to my boat and laid it in the back.

'Hope it doesn't weigh you down too much. But I'm sure the Guardhouse will appreciate you delivering it to them, Joro. They're fond of you and no doubt they've already planned your Retirement. Everyone among the Islands knows you're the best sailor we've had in ten years.'

Before I knew what I was doing I leaned forward and hugged him warmly. I would likely never see Poro again, and he had been the closest thing to a *father* that any of us had ever had.

We pushed my boat out together and I steered into one of the main channels. The fog was thinner there and within moments I could make out the shape of watercraft around me. Sailors heading towards the Matching. I was checking the waves for dark shapes when another boat rocked into mine.

'Bersho!' I whipped around. 'Don't ruin another boat, you fool. That'll be your sixth this year.'

'Oh, please. You crash one by accident and then it's just a vicious cycle. They only give you broken ones after that.'

He drew up alongside me. With his light brown hair and small, mischievous eyes, he was a reassuring face to see on such a serious day. He smiled at me and then let his gaze drift almost mournfully out over the fog.

'You know that this morning is our last chance for an adventure,' he said. 'After today it's either guardianship or Retirement. We never get to sail again, you and I.'

'Sinking ships, Bersho, in your case that's a blessing for humanity.'

'Joro, my friend. You've lived your life by all the rules and you're going to be Matched real well today. I've lived my life breaking plenty of rules—and plenty of boats—but had nothing but fun. There's one last place we should visit together. The Northern Islands. The External Zones.'

I tried not to look interested. But he was right that it would be our last chance for adventure together as friends. Our last chance, even, for sailing.

'The Northern Islands?' I asked.

He gave a small smile. 'I'd been hearing rumours of a massive island in the north. The Guardhouse never talks about it. Some younger sailors have drifted past it, seen a kind of monster and never had the courage to land. Well, I landed there, and it's not what you'd expect. In fact, there's someone there you should meet. Someone who may take us away from all of this.'

'This sounds like a tall tale.' I raised my eyebrow.

His face darkened. 'Two weeks ago, we thought that monsters in the sea were a tall tale. And now Tenko is gone. I don't blame you for not trusting me. I certainly don't trust the Guardhouse and their promises of safety anymore.'

I'd let my boat steer north without meaning to, towards the island that Bersho wanted to visit. My mind was sodden with indecision. Bersho was right: the Guardhouse had always denied the existence of monsters, and their words had felt like an anchor of truth until two weeks ago. Who did I trust more, the Guardhouse or my friend?

'Who's on the island, and why should I meet them?' I asked.

He laughed. 'I doubt you'd believe me if I told you. But the island is close, not more than half an hour away if we move fast—'

He was cut off. A light beamed out of the swirling mists around us and passed swiftly over Bersho's boat.

'Command from the Ocean Guard!' howled a voice. 'Turn your ship eastwards to rejoin the fleet. You are nearing an External Zone. I repeat, turn eastwards.'

'"Your ship"?' Bersho snorted. 'The silly fellow thinks there's only one of us.' He looked at me and nodded. 'Go on. Get to the island. I'll go to the Matching and make an excuse for you. Go and have our adventure, my friend. Perhaps I'll hear all about it at the Ceremony later.'

Before I could protest, he had turned his boat into the wind and sped off towards the Ocean Guard, calling out to him. 'Good morning, guardian! I was taking one last look at the freedom of the high seas before I'm carted off to matrimony. Old geezer like yourself, I'm sure you can sympathise.'

The light flashed out again, spurring me to move. I grabbed hold of my lines and tacked into the wind, pressing north. I hardly knew what I was doing, but Bersho was right; before long a great headland reared up before me, visible even in the mist. It cantered down to a low bay floored with yellow sand, which twisted up to a green hill thinly covered with fog.

My boat drifted onto the sand and I stepped out. I did not know whether to believe Bersho about the person I was to meet, but something curious in me wanted to see the forbidden place. I leaned against the keel, resting my arms, then looked about. Bersho had mentioned a monster … Eventually, I made out in the mists ahead two red eyes. They shone like distant embers in the fog, and as the mists swirled I saw that they glared out of a great and spiky brown face. Fear knotted my stomach and I froze, but after five minutes the eyes had still not blinked or moved.

'Is that a propeller?' asked a voice. 'God, I could use one of those.'

A figure stepped from the mist. I jumped back, but they moved straight past me to the item in the boat.

'It's water-damaged, certainly,' they continued, 'but it might be useable. Plenty of rust, but what can you expect? The blades are still set strongly to the hub.'

The figure was strikingly dressed, their voice strange, and suddenly I realised that I was in the presence of a lady.

We sailors wore heavy, knitted jumpers and thick pants made from seaweed and local grasses we collected. We'd been told that ladies were willowy, elegant creatures in silk gowns and dresses that shimmered like the emerald fish that darted between the seagrasses.

But this girl was clad head-to-toe in a heavy type of clothing Poro had told me about once: leather. It was made of the skins of animals that didn't exist anymore and was renowned for its toughness. Good leather, Poro said, was strong enough to survive the cut of a weak knife, could warmly protect its wearer against the cold and rain, and yet was flexible enough to sail a boat in. I'd often wished that I'd had leather to wear during storms.

It was hard to tell the true dimensions of her frame beneath her bulky leathers. But it was evident to me that ladies were different from sailors. Our bodies were weighty; hers was lithe as she handled the propellor. The features of her face were sharp, well-defined—her green eyes were clearer and more penetrating than any mist-dulled sailor's eyes I'd ever seen. Her hair ran to her shoulders; ours was always cut down to the centimetre. I could not describe the alien way her voice sounded, except that it reminded me of shallow water running over smooth rocks.

'Here,' she said, looking at me. 'Come up to the house. You're soaked and you'll be dead within hours unless we get you dry.'

She was right; I'd gotten drenched by waves. But I glanced up at the red eyes ahead.

'You have a home here, on this island with a monster?'

'A monster?' She looked at me quizzically, then followed my gaze. 'Ah. I'm sure that for a young sailor like you, many things, like the lights of my house up there, will seem like monsters. Come on, don't be afraid.'

'I really shouldn't. I've already broken the rules coming here, and it's Matching Day.' I could already imagine the Guardhouse learning what I'd done, and withdrawing any chance of Retirement.

'It's Matching Day, is it? You're not so young then; we're about the same age. And you can go to the Matching but after a cup of tea and an hour in front of the fire. In fact, maybe this should be a trade. I'll give you the life-saving warmth of my fire and you can give me that propellor.'

'Alright,' I said, coughing. A chill was already seeping into my shoulders and my neck.

'What's your name?' she asked as we pulled the heavy piece from the boat.

'Joro, sailor of the Eighteenth Island. What's yours?'

'Lena.'

'Of what Island?'

'Australia.'

'What Island is that? What's its number?'

'It doesn't have a number. It's a part of the world that you sailors have forgotten. Before the War and the End Times, all your Islands were part of the much larger continent that I live on and the whole thing was called Australia. I don't think anyone lives here now but me. Guards used to visit, but no one's come since my parents died a few years ago. The Guardhouse probably thinks I'm dead as well.'

I had so many questions, about what *parents* were and why the Guards had never spoken about this island. But by then we had ascended the hill and the red eyes were glaring down on me. I flinched.

'It's no monster, Joro,' Lena said. 'It's just my furnace fires glowing through the windows of my house. It's a redder flame than you've probably ever seen in your Island fireplaces. Come in.'

She led me up a little stone path to a tall, square house. Many windows were set in the walls, and the wooden panels between them were carved in ornate spheres and cubes. She pushed open a grand door and led me into a wide room lit with candles. They hung from the ceiling on thin chains of golden metal, and the flames themselves were encased in a smooth and transparent material.

'They're light globes,' she said. 'I've found a way to burn special filaments inside orbs of glass. It's quite simple once you've balanced the metals correctly.'

I would have kept looking around the room, but she ushered me into a large hall where a blazing fire roared across a whole wall. I could feel it rather than see it—huge iron screens covered it except at one small opening. She brought a chair over and sat me down before the opening.

'This is the furnace,' she explained. 'Like a big fireplace, but for heating metals into liquid. The screens keep the heat focused inside. The opening is where I do all my metalwork. I'll get you some clean clothes,' she said, and scurried away.

I gazed across the furnace room. It had tables full of metal gadgets, some small, some large, and all seemed to shine bronze and gold. The room hissed with noise: fire crackled and roared, little machines shrieked and burst with steam, gadgets rolled and whizzed across the floor, and transparent tubes bubbled with glimmering liquids of silver and green.

In the very centre of the room sat a huge metal contraption with two oar-like devices coming out of either side, and I wondered what it was and why it had such prominence.

She returned with some thick white garments, which she said went on first, and then a layer of leather pants, vest and coat. She pressed them into my hands and turned away so I could change. I felt odd stripping down and changing into strange new clothes in the presence of a lady, even with her back turned, so I did it quickly.

'How big is this place?' I asked as I drew on the final layer.

She glanced over, saw that I was done and turned back around. 'Four storeys. It was my parents' house; something of a mansion, I suppose. I was born here. My parents used to take me out to the Islands every so often when they went to get supplies from the Guardhouse. But that was years ago.'

'Parents?'

'I'm sorry.' She shook her head. 'I forget that Island children don't grow up the same way I did. In the old times, before the War, people who loved each other would often have children and live alongside them for many years. They were called parents, usually a mother and a father, but not always. There was no need for guardians unless something unfortunate happened to the parents.

'Back then, people could become whatever they wanted to, not just sailors and ladies. My parents were inventors. They built things with their hands and then with machines. The Guards let them continue like that, perhaps just to see what they might invent. But they died in the mists between the Islands five years ago, picking up supplies. I've been on my own ever since. Some brave sailors come in close to my bay. But the Guardhouse must just think I'm an old myth by now.'

'And so you've been here for years, continuing their work?'
'Exactly.'

'But where did you get all this machinery?' I asked. 'Our boats are made of driftwood and grass. Metal is hard to come by.'

'About a year ago I found a tunnel near the house. I followed it for a whole day until I found a ladder leading above ground. It brought me up into a world I'd never seen before, something my parents once called a city. It was a mess of pipes and concrete, with thousands of doorways that led into thousands of different buildings. The passageways between them were filled with fog, but also with strange contraptions.

'I came across one, a big metal beast with four round little legs, and eventually found a way to break into it. I learnt how to control it. You turn on its eyes, which can see partway through the mists, and press a pedal, which makes it carry you through the city. Later, I looked it up in a book in my parents' library. It's a machine called a *car*.

'After that, I began conducting regular searches on the city. I could never tell if there was anyone else there. Sometimes I heard sounds in the fog but didn't know whether it was just metal signs clanging in the mist or towers creaking in the rain. I drove the car to new buildings and took as much metal as I could find. Then I'd take it back through the tunnel and work on it here in the furnace.'

I pointed at the bronze machine in the middle of the room. 'And that's what you've been creating?'

She nodded. 'It's an airship, powered by a steam engine. Something to carry us into the skies.'

'Into the skies? What do you think is up there?'

'Fresh air, silly. A world of blue.' She shook her head. 'I guess you only know about the sea, which is coated in mists. What an awful world, all that grey water and grey cloud. I guess you know nothing of greenery or sunlight, of the colour of vines on a spring day. Have you ever seen the sky?' She leaned towards a window. 'I don't think we'll see much on a winter's day like today, but I can at least show you the garden. Come.'

She took me through a short hallway out into an open garden. I had never seen one so large; my Island had only a small square of dirt for planting potatoes and onions. But this garden was as large as an entire island, and bloomed with all kinds of colourful plants I'd never seen before. One bed burst with startling scarlet spheres on thin green stalks, reminding me of red anemones amongst green seaweed fronds.

'Roses,' she said. 'And nasturtiums, my favourite, over there. This is a grove of wattles that I've tended for years now. They've just started flowering.'

She was referring not to a garden bed, but a whole wall of

trees that pressed along the little path she was leading me down. I had heard of these groups of trees: they were called *forests*. Trees were so rare on the Islands that I'd seen more driftwood in my life than living wood, but here the forest was thick in all directions.

I felt calm, as if the world around me was gentle rather than deadly, and realised it was because of the lack of fog. Mist hung above the trees instead of around them, and I could see everything clearly. Nearby were a table and chairs, and an old rock wall covered in vines, and beyond that were hills and open paths, which the mists left alone as they drifted towards the sky.

'I can see you're surprised,' Lena said. 'The lack of mist is due to the air that the trees breathe. They keep the circulation going, like big upright bellows.'

There was a great whooshing in the air and a huge beast swooped down on us. I ducked, but Lena just stretched out her arm. The creature landed on her wrist and folded itself into a dark, tawny statue.

'Don't be afraid,' she said. 'It's just one of my eagles. There's a huge variety here. This is a wedge-tailed eagle, one of my favourites. Her name is Arcadia.'

I could see the advantage of her leathers now. Her arm was protected from the eagle's tight grip by long leather gloves, laced with thick red string and adorned with gold buttons. It perfectly matched her leather coat, which was rimmed with gold and red stitching, and fastened securely with a black leather belt.

'The things on its back are called wings,' Lena said. 'They're like the sails on your boat. They catch the wind and use it to soar and glide. The birds here inspired my designs for the airship.'

She looked down dolefully and then lifted her eyes to

the sky. 'I have only the birds for company now. My powerful owls, my eagles. When I see them flying, I think of my mother and father, how they tried to soar above the world with their inventions. It would be an honour to follow their lead, to follow the birds into the great blue above. I believe there's a kind of paradise in the skies that only the birds know.'

The great beast flew off again. We watched its broad brown wings sweeping the air, thrusting it upwards, before it disappeared into the weak blue light above us.

'Here. Lie down with me,' Lena said. She smoothed over some grass and beckoned me down to the soft, mossy ground. 'Close your eyes and dream of a broad blue sky. Can you see it, thrilling and perfect? I know it's up there, above the angry mists. I've glimpsed it.'

I lay down and closed my eyes. Her voice changed, became more serious. 'I had a visit from someone last week. Your friend Bersho. The first person I've seen in years. He is a courageous fellow, though a terrible sailor. I brought him inside and we talked. He certainly loves you; he said that you should see this place. He said that you're the greatest sailor in living memory.'

She took a deep breath. 'So you can stay on the water. You can go to the Ceremony. You can get married to one of the fine young ladies and live on one of the Islands. I'm sure that life has its pleasures, but I don't want to stay around these watery swamps forever.

'I'm an inventor, and you're a sailor. I could use you. Just imagine being at the bow of my airship, soaring with the wind in your sails and the gears ticking below your feet. You can fly us straight out of the mist into the unknown paradises.

'Just think, one day there'll be leagues of us flying through the skies, people just like you and Bersho, in ships a hundred times stronger than mine. There'll be whole academies teaching people how to fly. There'll be cities in the air. Isn't it amazing to think of what the future holds, if only we're brave enough to get there?'

'But what would we find?' I asked. 'Here we have mist and monsters and the Guardhouse. What if there are whole worlds of beasts and villains waiting for us up there?'

She shrugged. 'That's a chance we have to take. But waiting down here for the Matching, the monsters and the mist, is death, either a slow one or a quick one. But we can sail away. Don't tell me you don't want to try. You've seen a bird fly. We can go with them. We can live, we can breathe. We can soar. Come with me to the blue and the wild.'

She stood up, tied her hair back, ready for the fluttering wind, and tightened her leather coat around her. I saw the golden buttons flash on her leather gauntlets, her brass fittings shimmered. She stretched her hand out.

'On your Matching Day, you have brought me a propeller and brought yourself, the greatest pilot I could ever have. Are you ready to go with me into the sky?'

The mist curled about me like a coffin. I could feel my back sinking slowly into the mossy mud and wet grass. It grabbed at me with all its might. I thought of the monster that had devoured Tenko, of the grey Guardhouses and the golden promise of long Retirement, of the mist which was slowly killing Poro. An eagle cried somewhere above the fog.

'I'm ready,' I said, and took her hand.

I was going to fly with Lena of the Airships.

# TO LIGHT A MATCH, TO START THE FIRE

## BIANCA BREEN

'I'm telling you,' Hadrian said. 'They're hiding something in there.'

Leo glanced up from where he was carefully peeling the plastic back from his dehydrated meal. Sitting together on the roof of the factory where they worked, Hadrian's eyes were fixed on the chimneys in the distance as he chewed his fingernail, sandy blond hair falling into his eyes. The chimneys, attached to neighbouring Kaneel Factory, cleaved the skyline like three black wounds. Despite being out of service for the past fourteen months, dark smoke curled from the pipes every few days. A warm breeze scraped Leo's face, sending a metallic taste to the back of his throat.

'And I'm telling you,' Leo said, returning to his lunch of what had once been something like mashed potatoes but had gone cold and hard. 'They've probably just hired it out to the Inventor's Guild. Apprentices, freelancers. That sort of thing.'

Leo felt, rather than saw, Hadrian side-eye him. And he

knew what the look meant. They'd been friends since they were eight; seven years of the look. *That's just what you want to think.* Of course it was. He didn't want any trouble, didn't want to believe in any sinister plots. But Hadrian was practically vibrating beside him and it didn't matter what Leo thought or said. He just didn't want to get involved in whatever Hadrian was planning. He couldn't.

Leo finished his bland meal and packed his mealbox away as the factory whistle blew, signalling five minutes until the end of the lunch break.

Hadrian remained where he sat, chewing thoughtfully, eyes still narrowed on Kaneel Factory. Leo couldn't wait for him. Hadrian knew the rules.

Sure enough, as Leo re-entered Sweene & Sons Factory, one of the Actions—Conqueror Seki's personal guard, marked by their metal masks—fixed Leo with a stare. The man gave a short, acknowledging nod. Leo didn't return it.

He returned to his workbench. The metal sheets that crossed his bench each day were measured to size before being transported to another factory to form part of the oxygen turbines that made the air breathable on the planet of Bellona. Leo had only ever seen photos of trees, and the way planet Earth had been green and blue before it was destroyed by the Death Comet a few hundred years ago. The oxygen turbines were designed to look like trees, the blades painted dark green, the support tower brown and textured like bark, though Leo knew to touch one would reveal its cold smoothness. They could never replace the beauty of the real thing.

But production rates were dropping. Fewer sheets crossed his workbench every month. As one of the earliest factories established on the planet, most of the equipment at Sweene & Sons was outdated and struggling to keep up with the newer technology in the factories closer to the capital. This made Leo nervous; anything deemed useless by the conqueror was swiftly removed.

Hadrian returned right on the last warning bell, sauntering in without a glance at the Actions. Leo watched enviously as Hadrian took his place behind his bench, a few rows across from him. What he wouldn't give to have Hadrian's confidence, his carelessness, his ease. And not the fear, the prosthetic leg, the heaviness that Leo lived with every day. Hadrian still had his mum, his home. Leo had neither of those things.

But that was what happened when a conqueror invaded the planet and threw a coup against your royal family.

When the whistle sounded hours later to signal the end of the long, hot working day, Leo and the other factory workers lined up before the Actions at the door to receive their *ki* for the day—both sides of the coins stamped with Conqueror Seki's bald-headed profile—and have their pockets checked for stolen parts. To steal from the factories was to sabotage production—to steal from the conqueror himself.

They saluted the portrait of Conqueror Seki. Leo swallowed as he lifted his hand. It felt as if the conqueror's eyes bore down directly on him, a constant reminder that Leo had been kept alive only to be made an example of for traitors and rebels. His survival was conditional. Then he walked with Hadrian to the station, where a rickety train would weave its way down to the bottom of the nearby Rendip Quarry and deposit Hadrian at his mother's house.

The townhouse in the middle of Balthasar that Leo called home was tall, dilapidated and red-turned-brown-because-of-the-pollution brick, like most of the buildings in Balthasar's central streets. He shared the cramped townhouse with the elderly overseer of Sweene & Sons Factory, Bertram Peller.

When Seki had killed Leo's parents eight years ago, he'd been shoved into Peller's unwelcoming arms at only seven years old. Though Peller was elderly—much older than the twenty to thirty-year-old Actions Seki usually kept by his side—he was one of Seki's closest acquaintances (Seki didn't have friends). Leo thought it was a pretty poor thank-you for your services to be sent to live and work at the factories.

But Peller's loyalty meant that he could be trusted to keep an eye on a prisoner like Leo. And Leo was meant to be grateful that he *was* just a prisoner, content that he had lost a leg and not his head, content that he wore a black *T* for traitor on his prosthetic, and not a noose around his neck.

Peller was already home; Leo could hear the television playing in the other room. He limped up the stairs to his room—empty but for a single bed, wardrobe and desk. Empty of warmth. Empty of feeling. Empty as Leo.

He sat on the bed and removed his prosthetic leg, exposing the shiny red skin around his knee. The attack on his family's palace during Seki's coup may not have cost him his life, but he hadn't emerged unscathed. Only being allowed to wear prosthetics that marked him as a traitor was just an added bonus. He heard Peller climb the stairs and creak down the hall to his room.

As Leo lay down, a tap sounded at his window. He froze, heart in his throat, blood cold. Was this it? Had Seki finally sent assassins to kill him swiftly and silently in the night? And Leo would die as he lived—without fuss, without fight.

'Leo,' a familiar voice hissed.

Assassins wouldn't tap at the window. *You're so stupid. You're not even worth the travel costs to send a killer down here.*

He threw the blanket back and hopped the short distance to the window, using one hand to brace against the wall and the other to fumble with the window latch so Hadrian could stick his head in. Though Leo's apartment was on the second floor, the building had enough loose bricks that Hadrian could easily climb; a by-product of the frantic flurry of buildings for refugees after the Death Comet had destroyed Earth.

'What are you doing?' Leo whispered, shivering against the chill that crept in from the night.

'I need Peller's master key.'

'For what?'

'I'm busting into Kaneel.'

Leo suppressed a groan. 'Is it still *busting in* if you've got a key?'

'All the windows and doors are boarded up,' Hadrian replied. 'And the walls are too hard to climb. I've just come from there.'

Of course he had.

'I don't want anything to do with this,' Leo said. 'You know I can't get involved.'

'Yeah, I know,' Hadrian said flatly, pushing the window all the way up with his shoulders. 'But getting a key from Peller is going to save me so much time, and lucky for me, you live with him.'

Leo hopped back to let Hadrian slither in.

'Down the hall, right?'

Hadrian walked out of the room without waiting for a reply, which was just as well. The less Leo was involved in Hadrian's scheme, the less he could be incriminated by association. He sat on the end of his bed, picking at the nails on his hand, waiting. It wasn't the first time Hadrian had climbed the road out of the quarry into Balthasar. It wasn't the first time he'd done something stupid, either. Leo pulled his prosthetic back on, wincing as it rubbed at his raw skin.

There was a loud thump, like something heavy had dropped. Leo cringed, holding his breath as he listened. What had Hadrian bumped into?

Peller's snoring continued. Hadrian's footsteps did not.

Leo stuck his head out into the hallway and whispered Hadrian's name.

No response.

He edged out into the hallway, walking on a slight angle to avoid the squeaking of his prosthetic, though Peller's snoring still roared from his bedroom.

Hadrian was a dark hump on the floor, twitching. Another fit. Leo rushed over, dropping to his knees beside him, hands hovering above Hadrian's shaking body.

'Hadrian? Hadrian, it's okay.'

Eventually Hadrian stopped convulsing, though his chest rose and fell rapidly. His lids fluttered, eyeballs zooming beneath them for a moment, then he opened them. Sweat coated his brow and his blond hair turned brown where it stuck to his skin.

'Are you all right?'

Hadrian sat up, nudging Leo aside. 'Yep, fine.'

Hadrian seemed to recover faster than Leo. He was already pushing to his feet like nothing had happened, though his legs wobbled and his breath hitched. But the image was imprinted onto Leo's eyes—Hadrian shaking on the ground. He thought

Hadrian had come good for the last few months. What if that happened again when he was in Kaneel?

Hadrian disappeared back into Leo's bedroom. Leo followed him. 'Stop. Wait.'

Hadrian stopped by the window, glancing back at Leo.

'I'm coming with you.' His stomach swirled and he wished he could suck the words back in. What if Seki found out? If Peller noticed him missing or an Action saw him? Even the slightest of Leo's movements was reported to Seki. Nothing he did went unnoticed.

But Hadrian meant more to him than Seki's ire. And as a grin split Hadrian's face that made Leo's heart flutter, he knew he'd made the right decision.

Hadrian said, 'Let's go, then.'

\*\*\*

Balthasar might have been empty of people in the evenings, but it wasn't quiet. The whirr of nearby oxygen turbines, the rumble of factory chimneys, the slight hum from the sleeping machines … it felt to Leo as if the city itself breathed.

Kaneel Factory loomed ahead on the hill. Without nearby streetlights or Bellona's two moons bright in the sky, the factory was a black bruise against the dark. They closed the distance to the factory, passing its boarded windows before reaching the scuffed metal door. Hadrian retrieved Peller's key from his pocket and twisted it in the lock. The tall door opened with a groan that set Leo's teeth on edge.

The air inside of the factory was stifling—the machines

recently in use, the coals of the furnaces still warm. *It doesn't mean anything*, Leo told himself. Apprentices or freelancers, like he'd tried to explain to Hadrian.

Hadrian strode into the room. Leo stayed by the door, scanning the room. Humped shapes were scattered around—some only knee-height, others nearly reaching the grimy ceiling. The factory was probably filled with machines, either still in use or dumped here once they were of no use to the other factories.

The back of Leo's neck prickled, like he was being watched.

A white light flared to life as Hadrian shone a torch around. It didn't quite reach the entrance where Leo still hovered, but it was enough for him to start examining the nearby worktables.

'Oh, Angels,' Hadrian said.

Leo glanced up and his stomach disappeared.

Hadrian was by the torso of half an automaton. The machine was so big its metal box of a head reached the top of the factory ceiling.

Hadrian circled it, head tipped back to take in the massive structure. 'Would you look at the size of this thing?' Instead of fear or concern, mad excitement was in his voice. 'I knew they were doing something in here.'

Leo shuffled in two steps, then stopped. His throat felt thick, clogged with the hot smell of metal, with fear. He tore his eyes away towards a nearby workbench, to the loose sheets of paper. Blueprints, contracts … then a name he recognised. He picked the documents up.

One sheet detailed the slow but steady decline of production of Sweene & Sons Factory; another, an aerial view of Balthasar and Rendip Quarry. The third, a computerised model of a city layout.

Leo knew Seki by now, could read what wasn't said. Conqueror Seki wanted to destroy Balthasar and the quarry and make room for something else. Wanted to do it in a way that would cause the most destruction.

This automaton was a weapon.

'Hadrian,' he whispered through a dry mouth. 'Get away from it.'

But Hadrian either didn't hear or ignored him and continued to circle, occasionally kicking the torso with a dull echoing *thunk* that made Leo flinch. He was so on edge, so alert, that when the automaton made the slightest movement, he saw it.

'Look out!'

But Hadrian couldn't move fast enough, or maybe he was never going to be a match for the automaton. It brought its massive fist down, clipping Hadrian's arm, before crashing to the concrete floor with a force that shook the grimy windows. Hadrian let out a cry and rolled behind workbenches and crates, out of sight, though still in bashing distance. The automaton slowly swivelled its great metallic head, searching.

*Oh, Angels.* If it found Hadrian, it would crush him. But Leo couldn't get over there in time, his prosthetic wouldn't allow it, and what could he do, anyway? His hands twitched by his sides. *Think, think, think.*

As the automaton swivelled its head to the left, Leo caught sight of a glowing button—the only sign of any control he could see. It pulsed poison green. Leo glanced around for something, any sign of what he should do, when his eyes alighted on a hammer on the bench beside him. He picked it up, almost dropping it due to the sweatiness of his palms, and threw it with what little strength he had.

To his shock, the hammer spun until it hit the neck of the automaton with a loud *clang*. The green light flickered and the automaton stilled. He didn't hesitate; he loped towards a dazed Hadrian without taking his eyes from the automaton. He hooked his arms under Hadrian's armpits and pulled, moving quicker than he had thought possible, quicker than he thought his prosthetic leg would allow. Was it adrenaline or had the prosthetic always allowed him the movement?

He dragged Hadrian through the door and into the night before finally stopping long enough to glance up. The automaton didn't make a move to follow. It stared at Leo, then slowly sat back and resumed the position they had found it in, still once more. If it weren't for the painful pounding of Leo's heart or the blood on Hadrian's arm, he might have thought he'd imagined it.

Hadrian stirred in Leo's arms for the second time that night. He tried to stand, hissing as the pain of his arm finally registered.

'Whoa, that thing was *insane*. What's it there for? Who do you think built it?'

Leo didn't answer. The truth was too horrific. And what if the automaton had cameras for eyes? What if Seki just *knew*? His presence always felt like a sheen of oil on Leo's skin. Seki had ordered a dangerous weapon to be built, and Leo had witnessed it.

\*\*\*

The feeling of being watched followed him, even to places where he wouldn't be watched … probably. His bedroom, the bathroom. It was different from the times the eyes of Actions trailed him. When they watched him, he had never done anything wrong. How could he? Why would he?

But this—breaking into the factory, damaging the automaton, learning Seki's plan—*that* was wrong. It was a direct act against Seki. Leo had already been punished just for being born, for having the audacity to carry royalty in his veins. If he was discovered, he'd be killed for this. Seki would finally have an excuse. But maybe being crushed by the automaton would be faster.

He felt sick as he stood at his workbench the next day, eyes darting to the Actions and waiting for one of them to come over and pull him out of work. Before the bell had rung to signal the beginning of the morning, beads of sweat were already rolling down his neck.

Hadrian strolled into the factory a minute before the bell sounded, not a care in the world. Nothing hanging over him. Even with the bandage wrapped around his arm he looked as though nothing had happened. Hadrian glanced over at Leo and quietly mouthed, 'You look like shit.'

Leo grimaced in return. *I am so tired of living in fear.*

At lunch, Leo and Hadrian took their usual seat on the edge of the factory roof. Hadrian pressed the master key into Leo's palm, having made a copy using his mum's clay supply. Leo told him about Seki's plans for the automaton.

'I want to go back tonight,' Hadrian said. 'I'm going to destroy that automaton before Seki can use it.'

Leo choked on his rice. After he'd coughed until his lungs ached, he rasped, 'What?'

'You want to come with me?'

Leo laughed bitterly. 'Why would you want me there?'

'You stopped it last time.'

*It was an accident. I didn't know what I was doing.*

'I don't know,' he said. 'I'll probably cause more damage. I can't do anything right.'

'Did Seki tell you that?'

Leo jolted at the directness. But he didn't need to answer. He had never been good at hiding his emotions.

Hadrian swallowed. 'You saved my life in that factory. That seemed pretty right to me. I'm biased, though.'

Leo allowed a tiny smile. When Hadrian said it, it sounded brave and bold and so unlike Leo. But he *had* done that, hadn't he? He had moved faster than he thought he could, had used strength he didn't know he had. He hadn't frozen. He hadn't stood by and done nothing. And it felt *good*. Like perhaps he had a future after all. Like perhaps he wasn't the lost heir to Bellona he thought he was. The people of Balthasar and Rendip Quarry were still his people, and they were in danger.

'Okay,' Leo said before his fear could get the better of him again. 'I'll come with you.'

\*\*\*

Leo's palms were sweating as they approached Kaneel Factory. What if someone had overheard them talking about it? What if they'd been watched last time and now a trap had been laid? What if …?

'Ready?' Hadrian asked.

*No.*

He nodded and followed Hadrian into the factory. This

time, Hadrian kept his distance from the huge, scary machine and instead turned his attention to the stacks of metal crates and boxes that lined the factory walls. Leo approached the nearby workbenches, where designs and blueprints covered the flat surfaces. Maybe if he could see how it was made, he could figure out how best to immobilise it.

When he turned around to ask, Hadrian held a lit match in his fingers.

'No,' Leo said.

'We can't get close enough to dismantle it. I reckon we just blow the whole factory up and be done with it.'

Leo's heart gave a squeeze of fear. 'Are you insane?'

Hadrian grinned. 'Do you have a better idea?'

Leo glanced back at the blueprints and endless folders. He did not have a better idea. But blowing up the entire factory? He felt sick thinking about it. If they were caught, if Seki found out ...

He swallowed and looked at the automaton. This was a weapon. He couldn't allow it to be finished, to exact whatever diabolical plan Seki had in mind for it.

A tiny voice, completely unbidden, whispered in the back of his mind. *Those are your people he's planning to hurt. Your people he already* has *hurt.*

But Leo wasn't the heir of Bellona anymore.

Was he?

Hadrian gave an exaggerated shrug. 'Well, if you've got nothing better ...'

Leo stared at the match in Hadrian's fingers, at the flame dancing hypnotically, beckoning.

'Okay,' he said hoarsely. 'Let's do it.'

Hadrian blew out the match and they searched for gas cannisters, petrol, anything on hand that would burn hot and fast. They kept their distance from the automaton, eyeing it all the while. Occasionally, Leo was sure he saw the light on the machine's neck flash poison green, but it never moved.

Eventually, Hadrian found a few drums of petrol, courtesy of Aramita's Lubrication Services, and they both set to work pouring the liquid around the factory floor, across the workbenches, scrunching their noses at the strong chemical smell. Hadrian threw what remained in his container in the automaton's direction, where it skidded to a stop between the machine's legs, the last of the petrol glugging out to pool on the concrete floor.

Leo trailed his remaining petrol out the factory door and kept it going for about a few hundred metres, stopping when the buildings of Balthasar came into view.

Hadrian pulled out another match and lit it. He glanced at Leo. Leo nodded.

Hadrian dropped the match to the ground and they watched the river of fire streak down the road.

The factory exploded. Even from this distance, the heat of it roared across Leo's face, blowing his hair back and making his eyes water. The ground rumbled beneath him and he stumbled. Hadrian turned and ran back towards town, whooping into the night air as the factory blazed behind him.

'Are you coming, princeling?' he yelled over his shoulder. Then he pumped his fist, threw his head back and howled.

Leo ran after him, grinning, a lightness in his step. Nerves still swirled in his gut, at what they'd done, at the fate of Balthasar and the quarry, but the night had awakened something inside him, like the whirring of life in the automaton.

Though it scared him, he felt ready to face what came next. To take back control of his life. To light a match. To start the fire.

# TIME'S KEY

## EMILY LARKIN

The moment Desiree set the piano on fire was the moment Algernon fell for her. Even as it happened, his twelve-year-old mind etched details into memory: the buttery orange of the lit match, Desiree's midnight-black curls, her fierce smile.

The clock had ticked long past curfew, and they'd both be in trouble if anyone found them out of bed, in the music hall. Of course, if they were found, being out of bed would be a minor offence. Nothing compared to destroying the piano.

When Desiree dropped the match, its tiny flame flickered before catching. With a snarl and a crackle, a line of flames danced across the top of the piano and spread, spilling downwards, licking the black and creme keys. Desiree let out a wild cry, like a laughing crow, and Algernon gazed at her dark eyes, her smiling mouth, and the pattern of shadows the fire made on her face.

Heat hit him in a rush and he tugged Desiree's arm, putting more space between them and the smoking piano. Desiree began coughing, so Algernon gripped her tighter, drawing her towards the door. A smell of burning wood filled the air as heat reached after them. This scared Algernon so much he didn't notice his bandaged fingertips were bleeding again.

*Are you alright?* he wanted to ask. Instead he yelled, 'You're mad!'

Desiree's eyes watered from the smoke, but her voice remained bright. 'You'll never have to practise again!' Grinning, she added, 'The things I do for you!'

Algernon's heart surged, but his joy was tainted by panic. 'How can we keep it from spreading?'

Desiree's shoulders fell and Algernon realised that she'd never thought this through. When she'd snuck into his room and urged him towards the music hall, he hadn't thought her plans were serious. And she'd only planned destruction.

The fire swelled, engulfing the piano and spreading amber and indigo fingers onto the carpet underneath. Sweat dripped down Algernon's back. He looked from one side of the hall to the other, taking in the violins and lutes suspended from the walls, the cellos and double bass laid in cases on the floor. He'd never touched most of these instruments, but now these long-transformed trees were destined for a second death. The thought made him reel. What would the Earl say? The nobleman's precious collection ... his priceless vessels gathered over generations, destined to become kindling. In moments, the fire would ensnare them all. Would the Earl care more for the loss of his instruments, or his son?

Algernon could feel the carpet warm under his shoes. He grabbed Desiree's hand and made for the door. He tugged the handle, but the heavy door stuck.

Glaring at the door, Desiree shoved Algernon out of the way and yanked it. The door didn't budge. She twisted the handle; then, with a shriek, pounded her shoulder against the panel.

'One of the cleaners must have locked it during their rounds …' Algernon heard himself say.

'So we break it down!' Desiree snapped. She aimed another kick at the door, and when this had absolutely no effect, drew the matchbox from her pocket.

'NO! Don't you dare burn that door!' Algernon's imploring eyes seemed to reach her. Desiree curled a hand around the matchbox and let Algernon take her other, tugging her backwards for a run-up. They dashed, hand-in-hand, as fast as they could, and slapped into the door. Then Algernon was lying on his back, staring at a ceiling gilded in gold, threaded with smoke. It hadn't worked. This was rather like the time he'd accidentally run into an elm, chasing Desiree. He'd felt dizzy and bruised then, too. The tree won in the past; the door won now.

Did he hear yells in the hallway? Was that booming voice the Earl's? Would Algernon ever be able to shout—command—like he did?

With a screech, the door was thrown open and figures came barrelling in. There was swearing: language his father would dismiss a servant for using. Algernon was scooped up, carried. Someone was screaming for water; someone else was crying. Before darkness could engulf him, Algernon managed to ask, 'Desiree?'

\*\*\*

'I never should have taken her in.'

Those were the first words Algernon heard upon waking. He had spent the day in a narrow bed in the manor's sickroom, with clean white sheets folded over his waist and legs. One of his feet was bandaged with something bulky and cool. Coughs kept building and rattling his chest. These things didn't worry him so much as the fact that he'd heard nothing of Desiree. And now the Earl had brought almost the worst news he could imagine.

'You will have no more contact,' the Earl said, standing at the end of Algernon's bed. As always, he was dressed immaculately in a tailored grey suit, with a crisp white shirt and a thin tie the colour of pale summer sky. His height appeared even more imposing since Algernon was lying down. 'I am sending the girl away.'

Algernon swallowed the taste of salt in his throat. The Earl didn't appreciate shows of emotion. 'Father, I told you, it was my fault. I am sorry … I am so …'

'Stop mumbling! If you want to be heard, make yourself heard.'

'It was my fault! Not hers! Don't send Desiree away, please!'

'Stop yelling at me, boy! That's no way to speak to your father, or an Earl.'

Heat bloomed in Algernon's chest. He folded his arms to contain it but felt it rise in his cheeks, too.

'I know that girl has been a companion for you,' the Earl said, 'but she is *common*—and no amount of schooling will change her rank. I have extended privileges, and she has shown nothing but contempt for them.' A short, impatient sigh snuck out his mouth. 'If her father hadn't died in my service, she would have remained where she belonged from the beginning.'

'She belongs with me.'

The Earl's eyes flashed. 'Really?'

'I know it.' With a rush of recklessness, Algernon added, 'One day, she will be my wife.'

The Earl considered. 'You truly believe that, but you are wrong. Let me show you.'

***

The grand clock rested where it always had: hanging from the wall behind the desk in his father's study. Algernon had seen it only twice but, as it was rigged to a series of pipes, its flutey chimes carried to various rooms in the manor. Algernon knew how time sounded, even if he was somewhat unfamiliar with how time looked.

The Earl motioned him towards the ruby-oak clockface. Algernon craned his neck; the clockface sat eye-level with his father. The clock hands were thin silver spindles moving on a circle of old, yellowed parchment. The wood framing was carved into an intricate pattern of flower-buds and thorns. As his father clicked the casing open to reach the dial, a scent of dust and rich, old wood wafted over Algernon. He remained silent as the Earl swung the glass face outwards to see the clock's cogs.

'This clock has been in our family for generations,' the Earl said, slowly.

Algernon nodded cautiously. He felt exhausted and unsteady on his bandaged leg, but must not let this show. The Earl demanded his attention.

The Earl closed his eyes for an instant, before sighing. 'See here … You are too short, boy.' Reluctantly, he waved at a plush velvet chair in the room's corner. 'You can stand on that,

I suppose. For the clock to work, you must touch its cogs. Spin them, while you think of a moment. Choose a moment that you wish you could live differently. Then, take this.' He retrieved a key hanging from the clock's base. A long piece of twine hung from the key. 'Take this and turn it against your skin.'

Algernon had never heard the Earl speak like this before. He didn't speak in mysteries; he gave orders. What could any of this mean? 'What—?' Algernon began, but the Earl cut him off with a raised hand.

'It is better if you see for yourself. You tell me you and Desiree belong together.' A challenge glinted in his eyes. 'Prove that it is true.'

Algernon swallowed. He'd been asleep for what felt like days and was still exhausted. His bandaged foot must be burned … when he put weight on it, it *blazed*. His stomach was empty—he didn't know how long he'd been without eating. He didn't know how much damage the fire had caused and whether anyone had been seriously hurt. But he knew that his father meant to send Desiree away, and he had to take this chance, whatever it was, to stop that from happening. So, he tried picking up the heavy plush chair and staggered with it. The Earl watched, and Algernon felt the indignity of his father watching him struggle, watching him fail, even in a small thing. Panting, he lowered the chair, almost dropping it, and, avoiding his father's eyes, pushed it across the stone floor and in front of the clockface. There. This, at least, was done. Clambering onto the chair, Algernon bit his lip to stop from crying out at the pain. From this new height, he saw the spindly metal hands of the clock up close. Was it his imagination, or did they tick forwards, then backwards?

He touched the copper cogs, feeling the metal pinch his fingers. Why did the Earl insist he do this? Nobles did not concern themselves with how objects *worked*. Who touched clocks, other than repairers?

'You have to think of a moment,' the Earl reminded him sternly.

'I see …' But what did that mean? He had been told to choose a moment he would want to *live differently*. Would he change anything, if he could?

Of course. He would stop Desiree from starting a fire. If he could do that, then she wouldn't be sent away. Concentrating on this, Algernon spun the cogs again, took the key from his father's outstretched hand, and held it up to his face. 'Do I have to …?'

'Turn it against your skin.'

Algernon couldn't explain the jitter down his spine. He pressed the key against his palm and turned it. The clock hands skipped backwards.

***

'Come on, Non!'

Desiree was shaking him awake. With a wordless murmur, he rolled over, sinking his head under his pillow. Desiree didn't understand, because she wasn't noble. He was exhausted from practising. Music was a gift only for those of high rank, which was why he needed to spend hours perfecting minuets, even when his fingers bled and his wrists ached.

He snapped into alertness. Pushing the pillow off his head, he shuffled up. 'Desiree?'

She laughed: his favourite sound. 'Good, you're finally awake! Let's go wreck that piano, so you won't have to practise no more.'

'Anymore,' he corrected her absently. 'And we should not …' *What?* What was it that he had to prevent? There was something urgent he needed to remember, but it was slipping away, like a dream.

Desiree giggled. 'You can play *my* instruments instead if you like, but no more piano, alright?'

Algernon couldn't help smiling. Desiree liked to imitate the serious expressions of professional musicians while she rapped spoons and sticks against glass bottles. Her instruments were loud, and not exactly melodious.

She beckoned, and he got out of bed and followed her. As they crept into the music hall together, his heart began to thump. 'I do not want to get you in trouble,' Algernon murmured.

She shook her head. 'I won't let you be sad anymore. You can't practise if there's no piano.'

*She cared*, Algernon realised. She truly cared about his happiness, in a way no one else did. His gratitude for her was a honeyed emotion that almost smothered his fear, but he still asked, 'But how will we …?'

It was too late. She'd struck a match and was leaning over the red-varnished wood, and Algernon was realising that he loved her just as he remembered that she would be taken away from him; he'd lose her …

'NO!' he shouted, starting towards her, and the key on his neck swung against his sweat-drenched shirt. He seized the key and turned it against his palm again …

He was back in his father's study, head whirling.

'So tell me,' the Earl said. 'Did you prevent disaster?' A trace of mockery entered his voice. 'Do you belong together?'

Algernon heaved in breaths, fighting for balance on the chair. He swivelled his head from the Earl back to the clock. 'That was *real*, wasn't it? This clock …'

The Earl nodded curtly.

Algernon could not keep his thoughts from darting about like a sparrow. Confusion was melting away, replaced by giddiness. The possibilities were endless … if he could go back in time, then he could fix any problem! He would never have to argue with Desiree, let alone see her sent away!

Perhaps something of his feelings showed on his face, because the Earl said, 'You were going to tell me, were you not, whether you succeeded?'

Some of Algernon's excitement drained away. He could not meet the Earl's eyes. 'I … she still set the piano on fire.'

'Ah. Then you are learning. The past is something you can revisit, but not alter.'

'But … that was only my first time. I …' He was ashamed to admit it. 'I forgot what I was doing. If I could remember …'

'Do you think you could remember?'

'Yes! I could find a way …' Algernon straightened. 'Father, I want to try again. Please. I just need to know more. What made me return?'

'You turned the key again.'

'Then I did remember, at least a little. Otherwise, how would I know I was holding a key?'

The Earl opened his mouth to respond, but Algernon could not bear to hear him argue. The clock was a gift he meant to use.

If the Earl demanded proof that Desiree was meant to be his, then he would find it, create it. He'd go back earlier this time, years before she set the piano alight.

He spun the cogs and twisted the key against his hand, again.

\*\*\*

He was nine, and sitting cross-legged on the carpeted floor like a praying mantis. Laughter racked his body. Across from him, Desiree grinned. She was missing a tooth, and her face was flushed pink.

'What are we laughing at?' Algernon asked, which made Desiree dissolve into fresh giggles.

Eventually, she wiped her cheeks with the backs of her hands. 'Oh, you really don't know? Silly Non! Your father only *thinks* he's got both our kites. I hid yours and ripped mine in two, remember? So he's got two kites, only he don't, hey?'

'He *has* two kites,' Algernon corrected her absently. Wasn't there something he was supposed to be doing? A moment ago, he had felt as light as the icing sugar he saw sprinkled on his hands. Desiree had convinced him to steal some desert buns from the kitchen, hadn't she? He didn't regret it—they'd shared a sweet feast; the buns were delicious. He and his best friend were having a wonderful time—one of the best times of his life. So why was his happiness fading? What weighed on him now?

Desiree rolled her eyes. 'Why d'you care so much about talking proper, anyway? None of the town kids will understand you, Non.'

Her words triggered something, and purpose flooded back to Algernon. He needed *her* to understand. He was nine, yes, but he was also twelve, fourteen, twenty-six, and all the ages he would ever be. The clock had done something to him: he'd stepped out of time in its usual course and, in an instant, his knowledge of the past and future was so vast it threatened to overwhelm him. He knew so much, he could hardly remember anything.

'Don't cause trouble. *Please.*'

'What are you talking about, Non? Don't tell me you're scared about the kites thing.' The expression Desiree threw him was scornful. She thought him a coward, and even while Algernon tried to cling to his resolve, his nine-year-old self churned with embarrassment.

'I … don't want my father to send you away.'

'Send me away? He's not gonna *send* me anywhere. But, tell you what, when I'm older, I'm gonna travel the *world*.'

Seeing Desiree's eyes brighten made him dizzy. Algernon lost track of her words as she spun tales about far-off places some town kids had visited, with seas the colour of sapphires, and green fire that danced through the night sky. She talked too, of places no one she knew had visited, that she had only read about, with mango forests, and caves speckled with pinpoints of light like a thousand eyes of the heavens. Had she ever spoken like this before? Could she truly want to leave him? A fist clenched his heart.

'No.' For an instant, Algernon didn't recognise his own voice. It was the Earl's he heard. 'I won't let you go.'

She blinked at him, head tilted. Algernon realised his sticky fingers were clutching a piece of metal, but he didn't know why. Then he thought he remembered, and he turned the key. As darkness fluttered across his vision, he was dimly aware that Desiree kept talking. It was as though he hadn't left at all.

***

The Earl was waiting in his study, and Algernon looked at him with the sensation of waking in a strange place. He swallowed. 'Do ... do I disappear when I use the key?'

'No. It is as though your mind is elsewhere. It takes only a moment for you to return.' The Earl smiled thinly. 'Making progress? Have you something that will convince me?'

'She wants to leave.' He had not meant to say the words.

'*Leave?*' Disgust rippled across the Earl's face. 'Stupid girl. She is a *child*, with no relatives or riches, no skills ...'

Algernon's gaze swung to meet the Earl's. 'So you understand she has nowhere to go? You do not mean to make her destitute?'

'She is a delinquent and a nuisance. A very *expensive* nuisance ... one that has cost me more than she could ever attempt to pay back. But ... no. Out of respect for her father—gods grant him peace—I will not see her come to harm.' A look of puzzlement crossed his face. 'Surely you knew that I had no intention of turning her out onto the streets.'

'But you said—'

'I am sending her away from *you*, Algernon. I do not want her influencing you more than she has. For years, I have allowed her to act in ways that far outstrip her rank. I have permitted her to attend classes with you, to learn reading and writing, to provide you with company. But you must have known eventually you would part ways. She is old enough to commence work, my son, and you, you shall learn how to truly be noble.'

***

*Four years later ...*

Algernon missed his friend. He missed her through the lessons in etiquette, calligraphy, dancing, and dressage that had become routine. He missed her when he passed the charred music hall that was never properly refurbished, and when he saw the cook's children outside, running with their brightly coloured kites, the wind in their hair. He missed her.

He sometimes wondered if she missed him.

Desiree was a server now, he knew. Servers used narrow staircases and passages to limit their contact with the nobles. They wore beige blouses and skirts a similar colour to the manor's sandstone walls, only duller. This was to help them blend in. All nobles knew that the best servers were not seen.

There was no time to wonder if she would be serving at the ball tonight. Algernon had taken too long brushing his horse down after a ride—a servant's task that would make his father furious if he knew—and now must make haste. After allowing his manservant to help him into a suit, Algernon waved a hand at a necktie. The manservant looped the silk around Algernon's neck, tying it in a firm knot that made his throat prickle. With a nod, Algernon dismissed the manservant and swept out of his chamber, towards the dance hall. It would not do to be late.

The ball was a rapture of vibrant colours and movement. Silk gowns in reds and greens were popular, stunning Algernon with their overbright colours and reminding him of summer festival wreaths. It was a night of swirling skirts, tinkling laughs and conversations Algernon wished he needn't suffer through. He longed for one true friend to laugh with. His eyes were drawn to the servers, keeping their heads meekly bowed as they offered refreshments to the nobles. Among the beige uniforms, one heart-shaped face was familiar. Desiree's black locks were gone, her head shaved to ensure uniformity. She moved with her chin tucked, carrying a stack of empty silver platters from the feast hall. Algernon urged her, silently, to look at him. And, as though feeling his gaze, she did. The emptiness in her eyes drove him to action.

He weaved through the merry-makers and socialites and dancers, slipping from the ball, hoping that the Earl would be kept occupied. His feet traced a path he had not dared walk for years—one that was strictly forbidden.

He was returning to the Earl's clock.

***

The first obstacle was getting past the study door. Ruefully, Algernon remembered trying to break down the door in the music hall, with Desiree. That hadn't gone particularly well …

This time, there was no threat of a fire. That, he supposed, was something. But how was he to get inside?

On the other side of the hallway, Algernon glimpsed a server. Not Desiree—the girl's shorn head was coated with a reddish fuzz as her hair regrew. Algernon snapped his fingers at her, and she started like a spooked horse, before hurrying over.

She wet her lips. 'Sir?'

'I require entry.' He gestured at the door, and she looked at him in bewilderment.

'Sir, I beg your pardon … I do not have a key.' She swallowed. 'I'm not allowed to enter there.'

Algernon heard his voice, cold as ice water. 'Have you no

way of assisting me?'

Pink spots rose in the girl's cheeks. 'Sir, a server is meant to always take good care, sir, not to misplace any keys. But if a server locks herself out, by accident, then she might … well, she might use a slip of stiff parchment, sir, in the door crack to jiggle the lock.' Her eyes darted towards her shoes as if she had confessed a crime, and, for an instant, Algernon felt chagrined. Did she fear punishment? Was he becoming like the Earl?

Algernon gave a curt nod in thanks, which she took as a dismissal, and fled. After a few moments, he had a plan. He strode to the unoccupied calligraphy room and took a few pieces of parchment from a drawer. On his way back to the study, he avoided the odd guest loitering in the foyer. Once he had finally returned to the study door, he set to work. It was a more finicky process than he would have guessed, but, eventually, he had it. With a click, the door swung open, and the clock was just where he'd left it.

Crossing the room, Algernon saw that he no longer needed to stand on a chair to spin its cogs. With a deep breath, he folded the key into his palm, and twisted—and the clock hands leapt backwards.

\*\*\*

He was cross-legged on the carpeted floor, Desiree across from him. His fingers were coated in icing sugar; a sweet taste lingered in his mouth. Desiree told him they were laughing about kites, and laughing with her was so easy, it was painful.

Their conversation meandered from there. She spoke of incredible wonders she would experience, with no thought of what her absence would cost him. Algernon seared with the thought of being abandoned. But he must focus …

'Don't leave.' In his mind, he spoke with a young man's voice, but he heard something closer to a bird's chirp. 'When we are older, we will have the chance to go away somewhere, *together*. Until then, just stay out of trouble. Stay with me, please. Stay, and when I come of age, I will make you a fine lady.'

Desiree's eyebrows shot up.

'Desiree.' Algernon reached for her. She blanched and tugged her hand away. He was a fool and he had lost her again.

Letting his head fall, Algernon reached for the key hanging against his chest. He turned it so it scraped his skin … and the clock reappeared before him.

His eyes watered as he blinked hard, and rearranged the cogs. He let the key bite skin, holding his breath as he tried again.

And again.

And again.

Algernon returned to the study, only to choose a moment and step into it so many times he lost count.

Each time, he failed.

The clockface stared at him, impassive. Could he explore the future? What would it show him?

\*\*\*

A week had passed since the ball. Desiree was packing her few belongings while Algernon stood, helpless, in her tiny room. How could a woman of sixteen own so little? She had two shirts that were a colour other than beige. Her mouth-cleansing picks and cotton pillowcase were already packed.

His spine was a collection of cogs, slipping out of alignment until he was ready to crumple. He had travelled to this moment, yes, but why? They were both happiest outside, running with the wind lashing their faces. Why did they not sneak into the courtyard?

Of course. He was thinking as a child when they were practically adults now. Desiree's face was one he hardly saw anymore. Her forehead was skimmed with light lines, unfamiliar to him. Her figure was no longer girlish. And a man of his standing should never enter a woman's quarters unchaperoned.

'You shouldn't be here,' Desiree said tartly, rolling a white nightgown. A wicked grin—the one Algernon remembered from their youth—stole over her face. 'So I'm glad that you are. It wouldn't feel right, leaving without saying goodbye.'

'I implore you—do not go.'

Her mouth twisted. 'We both know that I'm no good at being invisible. I never wanted to serve! I am better educated than most *and* I play an instrument. Spoons and bottles, if you recall. Even a little piano.' Desiree gave a wry smile, inviting him to share in the joke, and sighed when he didn't. 'Non, I will miss you. You know that. But I would prefer to make my own way than continue as I have and feel more of myself vanish.'

'You do not have to vanish,' Algernon said swiftly. 'I am almost of age, and I shall marry you—'

'Oh, you shall, shall you?' Her eyes flashed. 'Perhaps you have forgotten the part where you ask me.'

Algernon bit his tongue. Must she insist on taking offence when he meant to save her?

Desiree's expression turned to stone and Algernon realised,

to his horror, that he had spoken. 'Save me?' she repeated in disgust. 'Be honest; you mean to save yourself! You are not nobly rescuing me—*you* are the one who is unwilling to face a future that I am not a part of. Because you believe that you need *me*.' She shook her head. 'A lowly commoner.'

Algernon had failed again. He backed away to avoid hearing more, tripping in her narrow doorway as he turned the key against the knot below his collarbone.

He barely glimpsed the study before moving on again. This time, he skipped further ahead.

\*\*\*

'Desiree, wait!' Algernon called from his coach. He had only glimpsed the back of her head, but still, he knew it was her. He recognised her posture, and her black curls had regrown. 'Halt!' he called sharply to his driver, and the coach he sat in jerked as the grey horses pulled up.

He pushed open the coach door and leapt out. Desiree sat on a tin box, a hat lying nearby on the ground. Algernon's breathing grew shallow. She was begging for coins. The bottles arrayed before her reminded him of drunks he'd seen on street corners. After all Desiree's potential, she had been reduced to this. The idea made him burn inside with cold, like frostbite.

'What has befallen you?' Algernon asked quietly.

Desiree frowned; he knew she recognised him. Algernon had pictured many reunions—some happy, some not. Never had he imagined this. 'Many things, mostly of my own choosing. I have a happy life, if you must know.'

Could she be telling the truth? Amazement must have shown on his face, because she continued with, 'I'm making my living right now. Or I was, before you interrupted me.'

Algernon took at the bottles again. On closer inspection, it was clear that they held varying quantities of water. And were those really spoons he saw in Desiree's hands? 'You play them?'

'Yes. I turned a joke into an occupation.' She shrugged. 'The city-goers seem to enjoy my music.' She locked eyes with him. 'Algernon, why didn't you ever believe in me?'

The question stunned him. 'I did. I believed, more than anyone, that you could make something of yourself.'

'No,' Desiree said sadly, 'you didn't. You didn't believe I could be anything beyond yours.'

Was this true? When Algernon had pictured Desiree's future, she had been bedraggled and despairing, scrubbing floors or lavatories for those of lower rank than the household she had left. He had thought of her tears rather than the laughter lines he now tracked around her mouth. He had pictured her in drab clothing—greys, beiges, and blacks. Now, she wore a simple cottonspun dress, it was true, but its cloth was a radiant red. Bold, like her heart.

When Algernon found his voice, it was very small. 'I … didn't want you to go.'

'I know. So you didn't help me leave. It was harder than it needed to be.' Desiree's lips twisted, but even so, hers was a lovely mouth. 'I'm strong, Algernon. I'm capable, but I could have used your friendship. There were so many times that I wished that the bond we shared had been stronger than a longing to make me belong to you.'

Algernon measured the face he saw against the images of

the girl he'd held in his heart since he was a boy. He studied the tenacity in her eyes, the slope of her nose, the tilt of her proud chin. 'You may not remember, Desiree …' He stumbled on the words. 'Indeed, I expect you do not. The clock does not appear to work that way. But I have tried, countless times, to make you fall in love with me.'

Desiree laughed without humour. 'I know.'

'I have tried in different seasons and years. I have tried to be dashing, to be bold. Above all, my feelings have been sincere. I have endeavoured to surprise you and I have done what I believed was expected. Yet it never works.'

The moment swung between them, like a pendulum.

Desiree stood, meeting his eye level. 'Did you ever try letting me go?'

'I should have.' And he turned the key.

\*\*\*

Algernon's feet pounded against the stone steps, heart pounding. At the top of the stairwell, he would find Desiree's door.

It would be proper to knock, but he could not risk drawing attention. He ought not to be out of bed so late or pushing his way into the servers' wing of the manor. A week had passed since the ball and, if Desiree left, then the life he planned for, wished for, would cease to be.

Algernon's hand lingered on the door. But what of Desiree? He was of higher rank, yes, but did his ambition outstrip hers?

The ghost of memories roiled through him. Had he tried this before?

He pushed inside and found Desiree rolling a white nightgown. Her cotton pillowcase was already packed.

'Desiree. We seldom see each other these days, but I miss you. Often. I heard that you plan on leaving.'

The shock on Desiree's face faded. 'That's right.' She added, with a burst of warmth, 'Non, I miss you, too. I don't think I realised what growing up would mean for us. I ... I thought we would always be friends.'

'We will be.' Conviction rang in Algernon's voice. 'For a long time, I thought that if I could keep you close, eventually we would live as man and wife of Beresford Manor.'

Desiree's mouth slipped open in shock, but Algernon had braced himself. Or he believed he had, before the moment became reality. Had his lungs turned to frozen stitches?

Every vicious urge Algernon had ever known spiked to life. He could find a way to sabotage her departure. Who did Desiree think she was? She would be *lucky* to be his.

But Desiree's reaction exposed the truth. He could no longer cradle the hope he had held for so long. In his youth, Desiree had liberated him. Could he not do the same for her?

Algernon held up a hand, not to silence her, but to beg her to let him finish. 'But I know that to keep you close for my own purposes would be wrong.' He spoke through the barbs on his tongue. 'Our friendship means more to me than anything. So what can I do? How can I help you find the life you choose?'

Tears budded in Desiree's eyes. She gifted him with a smile. Algernon did not reach for the key hanging from his neck. He would not turn it again.

The clock ticked on.

# SEEKING MISS KITTY

## ADELE JONES

Ships from all ends of the earth crowded the docks at Sydney's Circular Quay. Their masts tilted back and forth like a hundred arms waving slowly in the air. Seamen worked their cargo under a brutal Australian sun, while a steady harbour breeze made insipid attempts to brush away the stinging heat.

Patrick Felton, ship's boy on the *Zenobia*, eased a barrel to a waiting shipmate. His eyes strayed to some young people a short distance across the dock—two young gents not much older than him, and a girl more fetching than he'd ever seen, not that he had any right to look. They were amusing themselves with the spectacle of seamen at work.

His eyes danced from them to his task as he shouldered the weight of his load, so as not to be caught watching. Despite the sweat stains like a grey-brown tide about the neck of his shirt, and the dark, unkempt thicket of hair crammed under his cap, he wondered if the girl might look his way if he turned at the right time or did something important.

He didn't care for the pompous fellow at her side, who sported lavish multi-lensed goggles and seemed to dominate their conversation. The second chap appeared content to let the conversation flow without interruption, eyes fixed on the elaborate goggles of his friend. Felton had heard those goggles enabled one to see the dark as if it were day, shade eyes from the sun better than a hat, magnify distances like a spyglass, and enlarge specks enough to rival a microscope. Such a person was the type to travel on those newfangled flying steamers; the cost of that ticket would swallow Felton's pay for more than two years.

Felton thought it boggled the mind that inventors had managed to get such hulks out of the water and into the sky on the mere power of hot air. The balloons that dragged the vessels airborne had circumferences rivalling a small village. In recent years, before the war, the popularity of the flying beasts had mostly crushed the life out of traditional sail. But now those fancy flying machines transported poor souls to a destiny of maiming and death. The remaining dregs of seafarers, like he and his shipmates, were left to resurrect the nearly extinct art of working traditional sailing ships against the forbidding force of the ocean. Add in a recent Australian gold rush, and it was near impossible to keep able men aboard ships once they docked in Sydney. The risk of being shanghaied—involuntarily put to work on an outbound ship—exceeded that of falling overboard in turbulent waters.

Felton bent to load the next barrel and wished he were already on leave. Keeping an eye on the girl, he didn't anticipate a small, lithe form taking that moment to weave between his ankles.

'Miss Kitty!' he chided, stumbling over the ship's cat—*his* cat—as his shipmate rolled the cargo toward him. The weighty barrel slipped.

'Watch it, boy,' the bosun grunted, swishing his cane in a threatening arc that came near Felton's back. 'An' keep that blasted feline away, or I'll wallop her too.'

Felton flinched, more in fear for his cat than himself. 'She's lending a paw is all.' He gathered the small animal up in his arms and smoothed the top of her ginger head, receiving redolent purrs for the effort. Setting her down, he smothered a snort of amusement as the brazen creature took a swipe at the bosun's ankle as she sauntered away.

'Keep that monster under control,' the bosun rumbled in Felton's direct. 'An' pay attention!'

'Boy's finding the *lady* over there of greater interest than Cap's goods,' the sailor who had hurtled the barrel at him teased. 'Pales against your finest conquest though, boy.'

The chortles and backslapping that followed returned Felton to his last shore leave, back in London, and the incident to which his shipmates referred—the moment they claimed it was time he become a man. Instead, he'd returned with the cat.

He watched Miss Kitty across the deck, daintily stroking a white-tipped paw over an ear as she balanced on the quarterdeck railing. She was a right vixen, and he was the only one for which she held affection. Every other man had to watch his ankles for a swift scratch or bite when she was lurking, but Captain permitted her for the fact she kept the rodents down in the hold. Looking up, she caught his eye, and he saw a smug smile cross her mouth.

*Should've called her Lady.*

She was a brave mite and had kept him company through many a wind-tossed squall, and entertained when the doldrums snared them in the middle of the ocean without a breath of wind. That brief stint ashore seemed an eternity ago, such that he could scarcely imagine his life without her. He'd been a wee babe of sixteen, but now he had the wisdom of another whole year to his credit. Even so, Felton shivered as he recalled the dingy realms of the London sailor's inn at which he'd lodged.

He completely missed the barrel rolling at him as his thoughts slipped back in time …

*London …*

\*\*\*

Felton's shipmates chuckled and jabbed their elbows into his side as they escorted him to one of London's roughest inns. It was scarcely a stone's throw from the waterfront and he had little desire to be away from the ship, but Captain had given three days' leave a piece during their time in port.

'Look at 'im, lads. Pining for 'is ma afore crossing the threshold. Should've tossed you on that flying monstrosity that just made sail to the war, boy.' A shadow passed ominously over their group as the giant balloon hoisting a war ship skyward from the dock blotted out the setting sun for a full city block.

Felton shot the able seaman a glare as they crossed the cobblestone street side-by-side and stepped through an arched doorway, into a reception area of sorts. 'I'm not a scrap scared! Have spent m'share of time up the sticks in heavy seas. Naught can daunt me now.' But his palms grew as damp as sails in a storm.

At the bar, broken men wearing tattered navy uniforms glared at his round eyes and beardless face. A legless man sporting a sprung-jointed prosthetic cackled through teeth rotted clear away. Another man wore a makeshift monocular that magnified his colourless, staring eye as it tracked Felton's movement across the room. Felton writhed, as if bitten by lice.

Spying them, the bartender's mouth split into a grin. 'Room's all set.' In response, the able seaman who'd been riling Felton tossed a coin at the publican, who caught it in his meaty fist.

They passed through the bar, his shipmates remaining near him like a guard of honour, all the way to his upstairs quarters. The hall was strangely empty.

'This be your room, boy,' an older sailor said, grinning. The overhead lamps deepened the shadows below his nose and eyebrows, and reflected light off a metallic plate screwed over the place where his skull had once been crushed. 'There's a lively redhead inside, if you're game.'

'In you go,' another shipmate goaded with a wink.

Their laughter faded along with their steps. A yellow glow seeped under the door before him. *Will they know if I don't stay?*

Slowly Felton gripped the doorknob and twisted it in his fist. It shrieked as it turned. A squeal inside his head matched it. Still, he couldn't bring himself to enter. He put his ear to the panel and listened for any evidence of the female they'd 'invited'.

Two brawny forms appeared at the end of the hall, shooting Felton's heart into his mouth with the force of a cannonball. Thrusting open the door, he scampered across the threshold like a terrified mouse, and closed the door behind him. He didn't want to turn around. After some minutes something soft poked the back of his leg. He cleared his throat, but when he spoke, the words were high-pitched and cracked. 'I ... don't want trouble, miss.'

Still she wouldn't speak. Instead, she prodded him again.

Trembling, Felton peered at his feet.

'Meow.' A ginger kitten with white-tipped paws smooched her head against his ankle.

'Miss ... Kitty?'

And so the night passed, after which, Miss Kitty was instituted aboard the vessel.

\*\*\*

A clip on Felton's thighs brought him careening into the present as the barrel he was *supposed* to catch ricocheted off his legs and tumbled into the water with a splosh.

'I *said* pay attention, boy! You're not on leave yet, an' are making a donkey's breakfast of it.' The bosun's roar saw his cane come down hard against Felton's legs a second time.

Felton nursed his stinging flesh as Miss Kitty dove below deck. The girl he'd admired covered her mouth with a lace-gloved hand and whispered something to her friends, who sniggered. The jaunty one with the goggles had switched out the lens and peered in his direction, no doubt gaining a magnified view of Felton's humiliation.

Heat poured into his cheeks like liquid fire, enough to match the sun. Felton returned to his work. *So much for looking important.* Shaking his head, he forgot about the girl with her pretty brown curls and finished up his duties. Heading below, he readied himself to go ashore. Miss Kitty made herself comfortable in his shared quarters, skipping up to his bunk. He seldom did anything without the cat at his side.

As a final touch, Felton adjusted his cap. 'I'm off, Miss Kitty.' But there was no familiar meow. Frowning, he clicked his fingers, but in those few seconds she had gone. 'Miss Kitty?'

Felton peered under all the bunks in the berth. He searched nearby cabins, even poking his nose in the sailmaker's quarters, which was one of the cat's favourite hidey-holes with canvas swatches and plentiful spools of hemp thread. No Miss Kitty.

His hunt led him to the hold, which was a hive of activity. Climbing through an open hatch, he found men shuffling goods. Amongst them strutted Miss Kitty. Felton laughed with relief and scuffed her head with his fist. She leaned in and rubbed his wrist with her head. 'I'm off, Miss Kitty. You behave while—'

A stumbling foot found the cat's tail. With a yowl, she flew out the hatch. Felton scrambled after her, scaling several companion ladders before gaining the deck in time to see her bounding over the taffrail, onto the dock.

'Miss Kitty!'

But the cat was unstoppable.

Felton dashed down the gangway, his boots making swift, rhythmic thuds against the wood. 'Miss Kitty!' He plunged into a stream of migrants pouring from an unkempt immigrant ship hugging the dock and stumbled into the cart of a travelling salesman peddling gimmicky novelties.

'Self-polishing shoes, sun goggles, time tellers, wrinkleless suits! Get them now before they disappear. And if it's disappearing you want, you can purchase your very own personal relocator—with a touch, you can find yourself someplace else.' The man's shouts struck Felton's ear but were absorbed by the sea of bodies that made it impossible to move swiftly. He cast an eye over the peculiar contraptions on display, fascinated by the idea of a 'personal relocator'. *Probably doesn't even work.*

By the time the masses thinned, Felton was far from the ship with no sign of his cat. He kicked at nothing before making his way about Sydney Cove. There were a million places she could hide. He continued onto the Royal Botanic Gardens, where he spied some locals picnicking on lush harbourside lawn. Felton wondered if food may have enticed the cat to their party, either that or the throng of seagulls also pleading for scraps.

'Miss Kitty?' he called, feeling the frowns of several well-dressed ladies sporting parasols. 'Miss Kitty!'

'What do you want, boy?'

Felton came about. There before him was the same girl he'd seen earlier at the quay, only this time she was near enough for him to observe the summer's day blueness of her eyes. His mouth went dry and he croaked, 'I'm ... lookin' for a little ginger cat with white paws. You've not seen her?'

'Not at all. And I don't see why you think it is *my* concern.' She laughed, her eyes finding her companion—the fellow with the goggles, which were now switched to a darkened lens to shade his eyes from the blazing sun.

Felton scratched his temple and flushed, realising how grey and shabby his clothes were against the ruffles of her pale pink silk dress. 'N-no,' he mumbled, wishing he had the nerve to say something witty. But wit and nerve fled faster than the cat had. 'But ... it was *you* who interrupted *my* search.'

'You called my name,' she objected with a toss of her curls.

'How was *I* to know you were just calling your silly cat?'

'She's *not* silly.'

'Well, it's of *no* consequence to me.'

Miss Kitty's gentleman friend moved to her side and grasped her arm. 'Push off, boy.'

Felton had a mind to tell him the goggles made him look like a giant fly. Miss Kitty nodded regally as she turned. Vaguely, he wondered how her brow had not a dab of perspiration on a day so unmercifully warm.

Cutting across Hyde Park, then Pitt Street, Felton trotted onto George Street, back towards Circular Quay. A young woman on a dual-cogwheel travel cart rattled past, steam spitting over him from the valve on the small engine that powered the contraption. A grub of envy ate through his weary limbs, heavy from trudging. *A cart would make things simpler.* But he had nothing worth trading for such a luxury.

Shadows lengthened as the sun nestled on the western horizon. The light it cast was like the orange-red of wind-stirred coals. The air remained still, and humidity clung to his skin like algae to a rock. His search had taken him further than intended, with no sign of his cat. *So much for my shore leave.* He ventured to hope the cat had done a circuit and might even be back at the ship, but the thought of returning and finding her gone left him hollower than an empty barrel. Cat or not, with the cargo fully loaded, tomorrow he'd return and they'd set sail—along with some passengers bound for England.

It wasn't Captain's practice to take aboard extra souls, but word had it these ones had paid ample compensation for the inconvenience. This alone told him they'd likely be pining for those flying passenger ships carting soldiers to war. Left with meagre pickings, the direct passage of his company's ship to Britain had favoured them for this task. *But what do I care without my cat?*

He kicked again at the ground and picked up a pebble with the toe of his shoe. It skittled across cobblestones and struck something hollow and metallic. He crossed over to inspect the object. It was a mangled pedal tricycle on its side. Righting it, he could see where a steam engine had once powered it, but the mounts now reached up to nothing. The seat had also been broken off at the frame. Trying the pedals, he found them seized and the steering bars wonky, but the wheels still rolled well enough.

Standing on the small platform separating the rear wheels, he propelled himself with his foot. Air rushed over him, blessedly cool now the sun wasn't trying to cinder him. By the time he trundled nearer the quay, the shades of dusk had faded from the sky and buildings stood in the solemn grey of nightfall. *No point looking now.* Felton winced at the stab of melancholy in his gut and hoped again she'd found her way back.

Ahead, merriment spilled from a public house. The men crammed inside were singing at the top of their lungs to a cheerful tune from an off-key piano. Felton used his foot as a brake and slowed the tricycle to a walking pace. He was certain some of his shipmates would be amongst *The Fortune*'s crowds, but he crossed to the other side of the street and remained in the shadows. He was in no mood for gaiety—or trouble.

Continuing on, he found himself nearly all the way to Dawes Point. Occasionally he'd hiss, 'Miss Kitty,' but he didn't pause as he made a circuit of Walsh Bay.

'Boy!'

Felton's head came about at the shrill female cry. He planted his foot and brought the tricycle to a jarring halt. Across the street, outside The Hero of Waterloo Hotel, was Miss Kitty. Remembering her snub, he began to walk on, pushing the tricycle at his side.

'Boy, come back here!'

'What?' he barked, surprised when she crossed over to meet him.

'Fetch my companion.' This could only be termed an order. Yet her face was pale and drawn in the light of a nearby streetlamp.

'Fetch? Am I some dog?'

'Don't be difficult,' Miss Kitty countered firmly, but the waver in her voice was unmistakable. 'I ... need you to get him.'

'That over-indulged man of yours?'

'Jonathon's not *mine*,' she snipped. 'He's our hosts' son. We and some friends were out for a final afternoon together, but passing by, he spied someone heading in here that he knew. Said he'd be two minutes. Now *they've* all gone, but *he's* still there.'

'Why don't *you* go in?'

Miss Kitty's mouth fell open. With a sniff, she flipped her bouncing curls and strutted back across the street to stand outside the pub.

Felton sighed and parked the tricycle. Waiting for a carriage to pass, he followed after her, only to be ignored. Leaning against the sandstone wall at her side, he noticed the glimmer of a tear, like a transparent silver line, marking her cheek.

'Are you going to stay here all night or do you still want me to fetch him?'

'You're ... you're not scared?' she asked, her lips trembling as a raucous exchange broke out between some men within the establishment.

'Not a scrap.' Felton forced himself not to gulp as the unseen interchange inside the building turned to fleshy thuds, piled on by encouraging shouts of drunken men. 'I'll fetch him, for this ain't no place for a girl, 'specially at this hour.'

'Or better yet, return me home and let Father deal with him when he shows.'

'Well now, we'd best let him have his say,' Felton reasoned, feeling his advice sounded mature beyond his years. 'Won't be long.'

He disappeared inside, ducking around the fight that was now being broken up, and searched each public space and bar. Tobacco smoke clogged the air, making his eyes sting and water, which helped him seem convincing as he pleaded for information from the bald publican pouring drinks. Each empty look and shrug tightened an invisible spring inside Felton until he felt like a loaded pellet pistol.

And then he saw them under a table in a darkened corner of a backroom—Jonathon's goggles. The spring of the internal pellet pistol let go, snapping high-velocity beads of dread through him.

Snatching up the goggles, he returned to the exit where Miss Kitty was waiting. He captured her arm as he passed, drawing her away from the building.

'What are you doing?' She dug in her heels and picked at his fingers.

He came about-face and handed over the goggles. 'I think he's been shanghaied.'

'Shanghaied? What does that mean?' Miss Kitty gasped,

wringing the goggles in her hands.

'It means he's been forcibly taken to serve on a ship leaving port.' Felton glanced about. Gesturing with his hand, he urged her to follow. 'Word is, there's a tunnel that runs from the pub cellar to the harbour. If he's not come out an' he's not in the hotel, he's likely trussed up an' headed for a ship down there.'

They glanced towards Sydney Cove.

'What do you suggest?'

'I asked at the bar. The publican claims he knows nothin'. Some other fellow said your man's not long gone, an' was in the company of a couple of burly chaps. If they're headed for the quay, we might just catch them, if we hurry.'

'Are you sure, Mr …?'

'Felton. Patrick Felton.'

Scarcely had the pair reached the waterfront when a muffled protest was heard. It was like someone trying to shout with their mouth full of marbles.

This was followed by a growled, 'Pipe down.'

'Hand me those goggles,' Felton instructed. He placed them over his eyes and adjusted the lenses to magnify his long-range vision like a telescope and make night like day. Peering out from behind a building, he saw two sailors dragging Jonathon along the docks, towards a ship readying to set sail. His wrists were bound and his groggy objections muted by a strategically placed hand. 'I see him.'

'Is he alive?'

'Very.'

Across the other side of the quay he sighted the *Zenobia*, but it was too far for him to seek assistance from his shipmates.

Time was of the essence. 'Follow me.'

Felton clutched Miss Kitty's hand and dashed from the shadow of the building, to crouch behind a stand of baled goods near the gangway of a neighbouring vessel. The goggles were strange to use, but he could see why Jonathon was fond of them. And then his focus fell on a third man approaching from the nearby ship.

'Lads, I've got me a new treasure. Can test it on this upstart to save hauling him aboard.' He held up a personal relocator.

Felton's stomach sank like a sea anchor. Now was not the time to gamble on whether or not the contraption worked. 'Miss Kitty, we must move quickly. Run ahead and see if you can't interrupt them somehow. I'll come from behind. Keep your distance, though. I'll draw them away and we'll rendezvous behind Customs House Square. But take the long way round to ensure you don't get trailed.'

'V-very well.'

Miss Kitty's light steps tapped along the dock. The sailors were more occupied with their potential shipmate and the third man nearing them, than watching their backs. Felton was relieved by their distraction, for he was certain his heart would have given him away with its violent thudding.

As she skirted around them, Miss Kitty let out an almighty shriek. The sailors glanced at each other. 'What did you do with my cat?' she accused. 'I saw you chase her off.'

'Hogwash.' One of the men stepped towards the girl, who bravely held her ground.

'I saw you,' she insisted.

With the sailors distracted, Felton scurried up behind them and slipped a knife between the coils about Jonathon's wrists.

He sliced at the binds. Once. Twice.

'Hey!' The man carrying the personal relocator was nearly upon them.

Only on the third swipe of the knife did the binds loosen. Felton clenched a fistful of Jonathon's fancy shirt and jerked him away, but the two kidnappers caught up and cornered them against the edge of the quay. Water sloshed below, and were it just him, Felton would have risked diving into the harbour. Given Jonathon had likely been drugged, he couldn't take this chance.

'What 'ave we here? Seems it's a two-for-one deal. Captain'll be pleased for the extra hands.' The sailors stepped right up to them. Their body odour made Felton's eyes water.

The third man sneered as he too closed in, clutching his new device to his chest.

Miss Kitty shrieked again. 'Mr Felton, the cat!'

The men paid the girl no attention and Felton braced himself for a physical blow. Instead, the sailors started leaping about, turning the air blue whilst grabbing for their ankles. The personal relocator tumbled from the third man's hand, and in his efforts to catch it, he ended up tripping up his shipmates. The three of them teetered over the water, scrabbling at each other to avoid dropping in. Like a seasoned cricket fielder, Felton snatched the device out of the air, and hauled Jonathon after him into a run. Miss Kitty fled in the opposite direction.

'Scabby sea bass! I spent me savings on that.'

Felton, with Jonathon in tow, took off at a breakneck rate, heavy footsteps thundering after them. Felton glanced back to ensure all three sailors had given chase so Miss Kitty could get a good head start. He hated leaving her alone, but it was the best option.

Though they were making decent ground, Jonathon was not so light-footed. Grasping the lapel of his fine coat, Felton ran as fast as he could, lugging Jonathon into side alleys and out the back, weaving and darting, even when his charge stumbled. Getting ahead by a turn, he tore into an alley and yanked Jonathon down with him, behind a parked carriage. His chest was exploding as he tried not to give their hiding place away, and Jonathon's best efforts could not fully stem his own wheezing. Felton collapsed against the wheel of the vehicle as the three men charged past. Gradually, their footsteps faded.

When they made the meeting place, back near the waterfront, Jonathon tumbled down at the granite waterline mark before the Customs House building and clutched his side. Felton leant forward with hands on knees, gasping. He pulled off the goggles and handed them back to their rightful owner. Jonathon nodded his thanks, but he took a moment before getting up. It was then Miss Kitty appeared from the shadows.

'Mr Felton! Jonathon! You made it.'

'I'll be quite alright, Katherine,' Jonathon assured her, straightening and reaching for her hand, but she slipped by with the briefest glance and clutched tightly to Felton's arm.

'You're *so* brave.'

Felton stared at her hands clasping his elbow. His eyebrows rose so high the skin of his brow felt tight. Was she talking to *him*? He cleared his throat. 'Me? What about you?'

'I hope my cat diversion didn't cause you upset. What a brave little creature she is.'

'Huh?' Despite the success of their escapade, her mockery of the cat made him feel like there were stones in his stomach. 'You don't need to poke fun of her.'

'Fun?' She looked at him, agog. 'Did you not see her march up to those thugs and brazenly scratch and bite them into retreat?'

Felton's jaw sagged low. 'She did?'

'Yes. Why do you think they started yowling and leaping when they did? No sign of her now?'

He shook his head.

'I just hope she makes her way back to the ship.'

'Me too,' Felton said, only to have her step forward and kiss him on the cheek. It felt like he'd let go of a yardarm and was whistling through the air towards deep ocean water below.

'You're so brave, as is your cat. You both deserve a grand reward.' Miss Kitty smiled, ignoring Jonathon's surly glare.

'Hold that thought.' Felton remembered the relocator, still clutched in his fist. 'Jonathon, what do you make of this?'

The other young man took the personal relocator and studied it under the streetlamp at the front of the building. Placing the goggles over his head, he switched out the lenses to magnification and night-to-day vision. 'I've never seen anything like this.' Wonderment made his tone lighter, less overbearing.

Felton and Miss Kitty watched as he read some settings.

'Its action seems to be dictated by distance—one, five or ten miles, and compass direction. Let's try east-north-east and ten miles.' He unclipped a latch, letting granules flow from a reservoir into a tube that spiralled around a central column. The column began to glow.

Felton tightened his hold on Miss Kitty's arm and stepped back, drawing her with him. In his focus on the strange, luminous gadget, he didn't see the three shadows creeping up behind Jonathon until it was too late.

'Hands off me booty!' the owner of the relocator snarled, bringing Jonathon about with a jolt.

Holding the relocator away from them, Felton could see Jonathon was careful not to touch the glowing column. Instead, he kept hold of the device's leather-covered handle. The sailors were now within arm's reach.

An idea sprung into Felton's head. 'Do as the man says, Jonathon—toss it!'

Jonathon glanced at Felton and Miss Kitty, then lobbed the personal relocator into the air above the seamen. Three pairs of hands clamoured for the device, connecting simultaneously with it. With a shimmer and snap, they disappeared, leaving the personal relocator to drop to the paving with a clunk.

Miss Kitty squeaked in astonishment. Felton nearly did the same.

'By Jove, it works, except it doesn't travel with those relocated,' Jonathon said, stepping to where the device had fallen. It was no longer glowing.

'I'd say that's a substantial design flaw.' Felton gave a nervous chuckle as Jonathon stooped down and scooped it off the ground.

'I'll say.' Turning it around, he returned the granules to the hopper and resecured the latch. 'Could be multiple-use, but I'm not trying my luck.'

'Ten miles east-north-east, you say?' Felton did a quick

mental calculation. 'I'd say there's a good chance they're wet and swimming for land.'

The trio chuckled.

'Jonathon, Mr Felton, let us escape this night air and return home. Father and Mother must be worried senseless.'

Felton needed no further convincing. He just hoped the feline Miss Kitty found her way to the ship before they set sail tomorrow.

\*\*\*

'Captain's pacing.' The mate muttered loud enough for Felton to hear as the passengers were boarded.

Despite the headiness of his adventures the previous night, Felton knew a pacing captain meant an irritable captain. Worse, although he'd been back most of the Forenoon Watch, he'd failed to locate Miss Kitty on the ship. Everything in him hoped they'd delay putting out to sea until she returned, but with Captain in a mood, it was unlikely.

He eyed the passengers at a distance as they made their way across the deck: a gent and two ladies. He could see why Captain might be worried. They weren't exactly the seafaring type—or so it seemed, with the ladies hidden under elaborate parasols. Although he had no direct view of the man, the gentleman seemed just as much a dandy. Though Felton felt there was something mighty familiar about him.

'Reckon Cap's worried he'll not get a scrap of work out of us with them about and then we'll know what,' the bosun said grimly. His shipmates nodded.

Despite this dark undercurrent and his missing cat, Felton's head kept floating somewhere beyond the crow's nest. He'd arrived back at the ship, his every thought occupied with Miss Kitty and their adventurous night. In the dark, without mind of dress or rank, he'd found her a good-natured and witty companion. Even Jonathon had turned out to be a good egg, once he'd relaxed some. Yet, nothing could ease the gnaw of disappointment as he'd done a quick round of the vessel with no evidence of his cat.

Unexpectedly, Felton had been compensated for his trouble by Miss Kitty's father—and no refusal could sway the man. He'd promptly purchased new clothes and paid a visit to a barber, making him look most respectable. He could only imagine the extra rations his funds might afford whilst at sea if he could survive the teasing of his shipmates.

All daydreams dissipated as Felton was promptly put to work. The bosun seemed crankier and the mate sharper, and he wondered what was his crime. Having suffered the cane repeatedly for no obvious error, once they'd set sail, he swiftly located an unoccupied crevice to stay out of the way until they'd broken free of the harbour—and the bosun's temper had opportunity for a breath of fresh air.

Felton peered through a torn sail brought down for repair. It was folded across a crate awaiting the sailmaker's attention—an effective hiding place, whilst enabling him a view of the pure blue sky. *Like Miss Kitty's eyes …* His mood soured with the reality he'd likely never see the girl, or his cat, again.

The passengers wandered about and were already getting in the way. Each glimpse of their finery tensed his nerves, while the older woman fussed incessantly to her husband about hygiene and comfort, justifying Captain's brusqueness. *Should have sent them on a flying steamer, via the war. Then they'd have something proper to complain about ...*

Weariness twitched through Felton's every muscle as the events of the previous evening caught up. Yet he was determined not to doze.

The ship's boy stirred as something soft brushed his leg. And then he felt a delightful tickle against his ankle, through the slats of the crate. He scooped the purring animal into his arms. 'Miss Kitty! Where've you been hiding?'

'Mr Felton?'

Felton stood up and found himself looking into the prettiest sky-blue eyes, framed by glossy brown curls. Before he could catch his breath, two hefty blows with the cane snapped at his tail. The feline Miss Kitty went diving for the nearest hidey-hole while the other hid her mouth behind her lace-gloved hand. Heat exploded in Felton's cheeks.

'Captain's been searchin' for you all over, boy,' the mate barked, coming aside the bosun, who still had the cane hot in hand. 'Now I see you're takin' a spell not owed.'

Before he could take another breath, Miss Kitty's father appeared and placed a hand on the bosun's shoulder. 'Go easy on the lad and his wee cat. They are heroes somewhat, having last night rescued our daughter and our host's son from the fiercest of ruffians.'

The bosun gulped and his eyes darted from Miss Kitty's father to Felton to the mate, to the captain overseeing the exchange.

The mate cleared his throat. 'Right, in that case it be a double watch, boy!'

It could've been worse, and Felton knew it. Dear old Mate

had to keep face with the captain, but nothing could tether Felton's buoyant heart. His cat was back, and for the next eight hours, he'd have a perfect view of the world—and his Miss Kitty.

# THE MAP-MAKER

## ELIZABETH KLEIN

Pain spasmed through Iris's body. A groan bubbled through her bruised lips.

Her eyes, submerged in warm tears, glimpsed a dull light flickering somewhere in the shadows. On. Off. On. Off. So irritating. Her neck ached, but her head … well, a fire burned there too, behind her eyes, throbbing like a drum.

In slow motion, she lifted her head, relieved as the tension and pain eased. Something warm dribbled down the left side of her face from her temple, and chills seeping up from the ground beneath her sent shivers through her body, triggering more spasms.

*Argh!*

Something had happened. An explosion topside. Was that it?

A monstrous fear hovered over her. Its claws reached for her throat and as a shower of earth and rubble fell from the crumbling ceiling, it triggered a series of coughs and gasps for breath. Her throat was a burning pyre.

Through the scarlet haze, she managed to push herself up

into a sitting position, which was when she caught the sound of creaking girders overhead.

*That doesn't sound good.*

Her trembling fingers inched to the side of her head and collided with a golf ball-sized lump. Her fingers recoiled. She tried to think through the wild beating of her heart. Where was Pender with the map? Wasn't he supposed to warn them of seismic activity? Of danger? Never had she experienced something this catastrophic before, whatever *this* was. Something serious must have occurred above.

And where were the others? Lyrica? Hubert? Grace and Dane?

Cloyed with a mustard-yellow haze, the choking air forced her to lower her air filter and inhale the portion of clean air she'd brought down with her. Even so, the supply would only last fifteen minutes, normally enough for a quick dash to an exit and then the lifts if anything went wrong.

The burst of oxygen cleared her head. She noticed a figure stumbling through the fog. When it neared, she exhaled the panic that constricted her throat.

Pender held the tatty map in his hands, peering down at it with his haze goggles on his nose. He looked up, stifling a gasp when he saw her, his luminous blue eyes magnified by the goggles—a sophisticated series of lenses that helped him visualise the tunnels in 4D, employing the dimension of time, something her team valued.

Apparently, Pender had the ability of foresight. He was a reader of time dimensions. It was a gift few possessed, which was why her organisation had hand-picked him and each other member of the six-man crew with infinite care. No one knew each other beforehand. Everyone was a stranger.

Iris knew the order. First, the CEO located a map-maker—4D map reading was an added bonus—and then five labourers. While Iris had signed up as a common labourer because she'd been desperate for work, Pender had come from the upper class of explorers due to his skills. Someone important.

So … why hadn't he warned them, kept watch on the time element? Done his job, for crying out loud. That thought flittered through her pulsing brain as she struggled to her feet and staggered towards him.

'Iris, we need to get out of here,' he said, taking a hissing breath through his air filter.

'What happened? Where are the others?'

'I don't know, but soon more tremors are going to hit.'

'Is that what happened?'

He peered into the map again, lost in its complexities.

'Pender!' She raised her voice, heightening the throbbing in her head. 'Is that what this is? A tremor?'

He glanced at her and she didn't have to be in the sunlight to see how white he looked. How vacant his eyes were.

Gathering himself, he said, 'It was an explosion. We have to move. Hurry!'

*Explosion? I can't hurry. What about the others? We can't just leave—*

Ice wriggled down her spine as she staggered after him, stumbling over rocks, fallen timber and rubble, jolting her bruised body. 'Do you know where the nearest exit is?'

Infuriatingly, he wasn't listening again, just hastening away from her into the haze.

'Pender!'

He swung around to look at her, his face streaked with sweat and dirt. 'Except for the one up ahead, all the exits are gone. If a tremor hits now, that could go too. So come on. No more stopping.'

That explained the wild look in his eyes. They had run out of time and needed an escape route. Since Pender possessed the only existing map, there was no way Iris was letting him out of her sight. She hurried after him.

It took almost the full fifteen minutes to reach an ancient iron ladder which Pender, once he folded the map and shoved it into his belt, began to climb first. Daylight glimmered through the shifting yellow fog and Iris was panting hard by the time he reached down and hauled her up over the rim onto the cold ground. Breathless, she peered down the mine shaft, but all she could see was the thick yellow smog screening the hole.

'Come on,' Pender said, one hand on her elbow, forcing her to move, the other ripping off the used air filter and flinging it away.

'Where are we going?' she called, tearing hers off too. Incredulous, she stared at the ruined city around them, burning with fires. Billowing columns of black smoke poured into the air. Destruction was in every direction. She could feel her pulse racing, the headache worsening. *What happened while we were down there? Where are all the people?* Her shaking hands scrubbed through her short hair as she sensed she was nearing the brink of hysteria.

Up ahead, she noticed Pender stumbling through the rubble and she tried to keep up with the map-maker's long legs.

'Pender!' she cried. 'You know you're infuriating when you don't bother to wait.'

He spun to face her, shaking his head. His skin had taken on a dull yellow sheen, a little paler than the fog in the shaft.

*Maybe I look like that too.* The thought flashed through Iris's mind as she marched up to him and grabbed a fistful of his jacket. 'Why didn't you tell me what was happening up here?' she yelled, hitting him in the chest with her other hand. 'Why didn't you let me know? Why, Pender? *Why?*'

Warm tears rolled down her cold cheeks. Great sobs wracked her body as her raw emotions emptied themselves like a reservoir. After several embarrassing minutes, she stopped and wiped her eyes with her hands, aware of Pender watching her. Waiting for her to compose herself.

'Would it have done any good if I had? It was going to happen anyway,' he said at last. 'I kept us alive, underground, where the earth cushioned us from the explosion's full impact.' Then with his thumb, he drew a line down her nose and over her quivering lips. She flinched at his touch. 'You're alive because of my map, Iris. That's the truth.'

In the back of her mind, she knew he was right. Maps were the sole reason anyone could mine underground in relative safety. It was the sole reason she had enlisted her skills to work down here. She knew they made the difference between life and death. They had saved countless lives so they could work longer for the wealthy corporations, though not for her brother, who had died years ago in a cave-in …

She rubbed her forehead with the tips of her fingers as thoughts of her older brother Kris lit a dark corner in her mind. They eased the panic running rampant inside her brain. She looked into Pender's dust-streaked face.

'Now we have to locate one of the carriages so we can get as far away from here as possible before dark,' he said. 'Maybe find an airship. Keep your eyes peeled, eh? We need to work together.'

'What about Lyrica, Dane, Grace and Hubert? They're still down there.' *They have families too, who are waiting for them.*

'I can't do any more for them,' he said, melancholy creeping across his youthful features. 'We have to get out of the city before nightfall. You know that.'

Her stomach tightened as a dark image fell across her soul. *Jumping jacks.*

She nodded, relaxing her clenched hands, aware of the horrors nightfall brought upon the ruined cities above. 'All right.' She needed him to tell her what to do, where to go. She felt so lost. What she needed more than anything was her own map to find her way home, but she dared not ask him for his. After all, Pender was the official map-maker and reader; she'd be illiterate trying to read his. It was his task to get the miners home safely once the job was completed each day. And it was uncanny how he knew where to go. The best place to be, she decided, was by his side.

For a time, they walked together, and it wasn't long before a carriage and its horse came into view, both incredibly intact—and deserted. The carriage belonged to one of the senior members of the mining corporation. Iris could see his bright logo across the front headboard, the sapphire hammer and chisel, crossed like swords.

Relieved, they hurried towards it.

'Get in while I start her up,' Pender told her, glancing about. He opened the carriage door's latch, swinging the door open.

Iris hesitated. Wasn't this stealing? And where would they go, now that the city lay ruined all around them?

'It's all right,' he added. 'The owner won't be needing it anymore and I'm not leaving it here for the jumping jacks to destroy. Now, get in.'

Iris gave him a tight look. That was the name of the ferals that plundered the city once the sun set. Thought to be part-human, they were wiry, tall creatures with long, metal claws for grasping … and destroying. Jumping jacks lived up to their name—they leapt over impossibly high obstacles, laughing as they did so, sending terror into the hearts of those who were forced to travel the cities at night. Iris had spotted one from her carriage window once, leaping over a tall iron fence as if it was on a pogo stick, and the image had remained scorched on her retina ever since. They were the monsters that inhabited her mind as a child, that lived under her bed at night, that made the nightmares more real. Ever since the world fell apart in the great Global War, such creatures started to appear everywhere and the people who had survived were forced to hide.

She shuddered and clambered inside the carriage, grateful for its iron hull and the sturdy iron horse that pulled it. She sat on the cushioned seat and watched Pender realign the gyroscopic navigation system on the wall, punching in the directions the horse was to take—hopefully out of the city—and to safety in the outer, independent colonies, reached only by flying crafts.

Iris heard the computer-generated voice welcome them aboard, all the while throwing furtive glances out the window at the shadows pooling around the ruined buildings. Her gaze lowered to the plush velvet cushions and faux fur blankets. She reached out to touch one to see how soft the fabric felt when she noticed her filthy hands.

'Don't worry about cleanliness,' Pender said without turning his head from what he was doing. 'Just use it.'

Iris looked at him, then at the blanket again. *Oh, what the heck.*

She snatched the top one and drew it towards herself, certain she'd never felt anything so finely made or as silky soft before. The sumptuous fabric eased her shivering and she closed her eyes, grateful they were inside the carriage.

But as the minutes wore on, she grew increasingly uneasy and her eyes flickered open, shifting her gaze to Pender's concentrated look.

*Come on, Pender. Get the horse moving, will you? The sun's sinking.*

He was as slow as a worm. She twiddled her thumbs and stared out the windows on both sides when she noticed the lock button and pressed it with haste. At once, every window and both doors clicked into the locked mode.

'Good thinking,' mumbled Pender and he sat back as the horse began to trot in the direction he'd set for it.

Out of the corner of her eye, Iris stared at his dirty, gnarled hands and filthy nails as he folded up his map and tucked it inside his top pocket. She caught his whistly breathing through his nose as he stared out the window. He clasped his hands in his lap and turned to look at her, his brilliant, tanzanite-blue eyes mesmerising. That gaze was infuriatingly familiar, but just as the last dream before waking caused details to fade into oblivion, the memory slipped away from her grasping thoughts.

'What happened back there?' she asked instead, not meaning for her voice to sound so critical. 'Do you know?

Surely you must know.'

He shook his head. 'Why must I know? I make maps, not crystal balls. I don't see everything that happens. People seem to think map-makers can see all the ills of the world, when in fact, we see very little.'

Iris raised her hand. 'All right. All right.' She didn't want to argue. She had no strength for that or anything else just then. 'Look, I didn't mean anything.' Her hand lowered and she tucked it inside the blanket for warmth. 'I'm just trying to make sense of what happened and who caused the explosion and why.'

Still certain he was lying about not knowing, she bit her tongue and held her peace. She began to notice things about him as he sat there that she hadn't seen before, such as how smooth his face appeared with not even a wrinkle near his eyes. His skin had a silver sheen about it in the dull light—almost an ethereal glow. She blinked and he levelled a sugar-coated smile at her when he caught her staring at him.

As the silence lengthened, she recalled other things, things she'd seen during the day and had dismissed. How he'd stared at his map just a little too often and a little too long, certain he'd known about that blast.

*You've known about the disaster all day.*

She needed to say something, clear the air. Or those circling questions in her mind wouldn't find any rest.

'You said you saved us from the blast,' she said, 'so you must have known something. You with your special lenses.'

She was referring to the goggles strapped across his forehead, which he rarely removed and through which he saw the mapped world around him. Sometimes she observed him turning the lens and he'd be still for a time, seeing what the map required for a specific project. Pender saw the world in four dimensions.

'I saw barely an hour into the future, Iris. Our future,' he said in a low, tired voice. He didn't seem angry with her for accusing him. 'I … I never knew about the explosion until about an hour ago and by then it was too late to warn the team. I didn't know who would survive.'

'So you let them all perish.' Her tone was harsher than she'd meant it to be. 'Why didn't I perish with them?'

He swallowed and looked away. 'They were heading for the opening.'

She remembered. Pender had called her back to view a seam of nickel he said he'd spotted in the wall of the tunnel. Iris had gladly returned to view and catalogue it when the blast had occurred.

'The others were too far away by that stage. You weren't,' he explained.

She realised she was shaking uncontrollably. *This can't be happening.* Images of the others—her team—dying while she lived. Lyrica, the second labourer and Dane, her husband; single mother Grace and her father Hubert. All dead. Her emotions felt ragged and raw and her head still throbbed dully.

'What are we going to do? Where do we go? Where do we get food and water? Pender, answer me.'

He placed his warm hand on hers and lightly squeezed. 'Stop panicking, Iris.'

Is that what she was doing? She shook his hand off and folded her arms. Warm tears streaked down her cold cheeks and her lips quivered. *Please, let us be all right.* She felt so cold, her body so bruised and battered.

The sun's last glimmer of daylight winked out as it slid below a tall building and with it went the day's warmth. They weren't supposed to be gone so long and she wasn't prepared for the chills that arrived with the night. Exhaustion melded with grief forced her eyelids to close. In spite of her loss and the feeling nowhere was safe anymore, the cadence of the swaying carriage and the trotting iron hooves sent her fast asleep.

\*\*\*

Fiendish laughter jolted Iris from her dreamless slumber, scrabbling to clutch the handrails as something powerful smashed against the carriage. Airborne, the carriage spun wildly in the air before crashing to the ground.

'Pender, what's happening?' she screamed into the pitch blackness.

'Jumping jacks.' His groping hand grabbed her wrist and he shoved something metallic into her hand. He switched on a torch he was holding, its bright light blinding her as she tried to squint at him. 'Shine the light on them so they'll leave us alone. That's how we fight them off.'

Iris fumbled for the switch on her torch and swung it toward the thin, open slats in the window beside her, as Pender was doing at his window. She swallowed the drop of saliva in her dry mouth and held her breath, listening for the nightmarish laughter that came from jumping jacks just before they struck.

'Pender,' she whispered in a quavering voice, 'how long do we have to do this?'

His pale face turned and he looked at her. 'For a while,

'til they leave us alone. We almost got away without an attack. It's seven o'clock, so we had two hours clear. In the scheme of things, that's good.'

'But do we have to shine torches at them all night? Don't these carriages have lights?'

'Of course they do. I just have to figure out where they are.' His eyes searched the control panel before him. The next moment, he thumped it with his fist and shook his hand.

'What's wrong?' cried Iris, her chin trembling.

'It's locked. The owner has the key.'

'But you set the horse's coordinates. Surely you can—'

A deafening sound drowned out her voice—rocks pelting the back of the carriage like a shower of hailstones. Jumping jacks had surrounded the moving carriage in minutes and smashed stones against its iron body from every angle. Iris swung her torch wildly about, sending the creatures fleeing, their crazed laughter taunting. They were never far from the trotting horse, which they tried to trip, pelting either it or the carriage with stones. But the iron hooves plodded steadily onwards through each attack.

'We're almost out of the city,' Pender said after a long time. 'Then we should be all right. You're doing fine.'

*I am? Thought I was falling apart.*

Long metal claws suddenly latched under one of the slats beside her and, with a scream of terror, she lurched sideways, crashing into Pender's shoulder and dropping her torch. The claws yanked the iron slat until it bowed outward from the hull, revealing a dark, wicked face with sharp, pointy teeth laughing at her. The hideous sight caused her to freeze.

Pender shone his bright beam of light straight into the

jumping jack's eyes. The claws unfurled and the hideous face disappeared in a peal of unholy laughter.

'Iris!' he yelled.

Her eyes flickered and she grabbed the torch and fumbled for its switch, relieved when the beam of light appeared. With shaking hands, she shone it at the slats.

*They've created a breach.* She sat back-to-back with Pender, shining the torch about until, hours later, they left the dark, ruined city and the jumping jacks behind and headed for the open countryside.

Exhausted, they turned off the torches and huddled on the seat, too frightened to fall asleep. They sat staring at the dark, silent slats and the blurred, silhouetted trees beyond.

Pender cleared his throat. 'I want to show you something.'

She turned her weary head and noticed him leaning toward the window, pointing skyward. She shuffled over and leaned forward to look.

'What can you see?' he asked.

'Just a star.'

'No star is just a star. The ancients navigated by them, made celestial maps and told stories about them. Some even said they were living beings who could assume mortal form.'

'They did, did they?' she mumbled, suppressing a yawn. 'Know any?'

'What?'

'Stories about stars.'

'Sure. I'm glad you asked. I meant to tell you. There's a blue-white star cluster called Pleiades—my favourite, by the way. One ancient culture told of two fallen angels who fell in love with the women of the earth. One of the angels found a woman called Istehar, who swore she would love him forever if he would reveal the sacred name that granted him the power to fly to heaven. When he revealed it to her, she betrayed and left him and flew to heaven, never fulfilling her promise. She was placed in the constellation Pleiades.'

She gave him a wry grin. 'Angels falling in love. Nice story.'

Pender smiled. 'There are many stories about stars who came down to help individual people who had destinies to fulfil, but who couldn't survive except with celestial aid.' He gave her an intense look. 'The ancients also believed in miracles.'

She snorted and grinned at the prospect. 'I don't believe in miracles, Pender. The world is falling apart and there's little to see that's good anymore, let alone a miracle.'

'And yet you survived every danger today. I'd call today your miracle.'

'And are you my saving star? Is that what you're alluding to?' She giggled, rubbing the moisture from her tired eyes.

'I'm just a humble map-maker who happens to know lots of stories. Want to hear some more?'

'Whatever.'

As Pender embarked on more star stories, her eyelids lowered. Her head rested against his shoulder, aware of him wrapping the blanket around her, his voice low and gentle as he spoke.

***

A sharp tap on the door jolted Iris awake many hours later. She was lying across both seats with the blanket draped over her body. The other blanket was tucked under her head for a pillow. Pinpricks of sunlight glimmered through the slats, showing that it was day.

Again, something tapped on the door and she focussed her gaze through the slats on a man wearing a blue cap and a blue blazer. He was holding a wooden baton.

'Miss, are you all right in there?' he called.

Iris noticed a scrap of paper and a blue and white pouch on the opposite seat. She was alone in the carriage, so she scrambled to unlock the door, shoving it wide to reveal airships at a docking station. She breathed in the cold air. 'Yes I'm fine, but you didn't happen to see a young man wearing goggles on his head get out of the carriage?'

'Can't say that I did, miss,' he said with a frown. 'Your horse only just arrived, along with many others.'

'It did? What others?'

'Others from outlying regions where the explosion wiped out whole cities. Refugees are pouring in in droves. It's a terrible catastrophe.'

'But what caused the explosions?'

'Nothing's clear, miss. We've only enough power in the generators to power the food court and the lights. We can't get news out here. But some say alien collusion has backfired on the world and they want to anhililate us; others say Russia and India are overusing their nukes. Who rightly knows?'

Her heart fluttered with dread. 'What will happen to the refugees?'

'Don't rightly know, miss. Take each day as it comes, I expect.' He tipped his hat, a sign he was about to move on. 'My advice is to stay out of the cities. Head north.'

'Thank you.'

Iris watched him meld into the crowd of exhausted-looking people. Refugees. Transient people who looked as lost as she was. Her one advantage was the iron carriage, which Pender had discovered against the odds, even though it didn't belong to her, along with a few coins in her pocket.

She looked around. Where was Pender? When had he left her?

Her eyes shifted to the scrap of paper and pouch on the opposite seat. She leaned over and picked both up. It was a hastily scrawled message addressed to her.

*Dear Iris, this money is for you. I won't be needing it now that you're safe. Pender.*

She read it again, then opened the pouch and peered inside, stifling a gasp. There were enough silver coins, along with what she had in her own pocket, for a fortnight's worth of food and lodgings.

Why would Pender leave so much money to a stranger? They barely knew each other. And where had he gone?

She tucked the pouch carefully into her pocket and clambered out of the carriage, shutting the door behind her. Her grumbling stomach reminded her how hungry she was, not having eaten since yesterday morning. If she could locate a rest centre somewhere …

She halted and her jaw dropped as an enormous hologrammed name of the station appeared in the sky above— Air Station Pleiades.

She stared at the name with a slow, disbelieving shake of her head. Her skin tingled in the warm sunshine and she lowered her gaze to stare at the milling crowd of refugees moving toward the station where airships waited at the docks. She felt giddy and light-headed.

Inside the huge air station terminal, a medley of assorted shops stretched before her. There was a food court. People were everywhere. Iris used some of her coins to purchase a chicken salad wrap and a cup of coffee.

While she waited in the queue, she spotted a small girl with fair hair in shorts and a grubby pink T-shirt.

*Where are your parents?*

The thought flittered through her head and she thought no more about the child as she shuffled closer to the counter. She carted her food over to a corner and sat down on a vacant chair. Opposite was a revolving series of advertisement images on the wall. One in particular caught her eye.

*Specials on all airship flights. See the stars for half price.*

The stars!

She stared at the ad with a blank expression while she ate, her hand reaching into her pocket for the scrap of paper. Pender's farewell note. She spread it on the table before her, took a sip of coffee and read it again. Had Pender been her special star, sent to help her in her time of need?

She watched as a young woman wandered over to her table. The others by now were all taken. The woman gave her a hesitant smile before she sat against the sloping window of the shop, tucking her bare feet under her. In her grubby hand was a crumpled handkerchief and her eyes were red-rimmed, her face streaked with grime.

'Are you all right?' Iris asked after the pinch of silence had spread to an awkward ribbon of time.

The woman shook her head and Iris noticed her turquoise

eyes swimming with fresh tears. She blew her nose while Iris waited for her to pause long enough to speak.

'I'm looking for my daughter. At the start of all this chaos, we were separated when all the children from my region were brought to air stations. We were promised the transports would come back for us but then came all the explosions and no one came. We were left to our own devices.' She dabbed her eyes and her chin trembled. 'I've been searching for Adele for three days without any success. I don't know what more to do.'

'I may have seen her here. Was she wearing shorts and a pink T-shirt?'

The woman leapt to her feet. 'Yes. Where did you see her?'

'Near the food court. Look,' Iris said, crumpling up her paper and throwing it in the bin. 'I'll come with you. We'll search together.'

Tears filled the woman's eyes afresh. 'That's very kind of you.'

Together, they hurried back to the food court. Iris could feel the woman's renewed sense of purpose as she hastened among the crowds of people milling there for food, searching for her daughter.

In a corner, sitting cross-legged on the floor, was the little girl. Iris spotted her first and shouldered through the crowd, apologising as she went.

'Adele,' she called and the girl looked up. 'I found your mummy.'

She lifted the weary child in her arms and carried her through the crowd until a woman's voice called and Adele wriggled out of her arms. She watched her run to her mother, who hugged and kissed her. Iris smiled.

*Glad to have helped*, she thought.

'Thank you for everything,' said the woman.

'Glad you have Adele back.'

The woman turned to leave, when Iris called, reaching in her pocket for the pouch, 'I can give you some coins for a meal and a flight home.'

'I … I don't know what to say,' the woman said, tearing up again. 'That would help us tremendously. We lost everything when we had to flee. Thank you so much.'

Iris placed enough coins in her palm for her and Adele and watched them disappear among the jostling people. She then pondered how she would get home from there. Pender's words resurfaced in her mind. It was the oddest thing.

*The ancients believed in miracles.*

That's what she needed right now—a miracle.

Just then, the loudspeaker crackled. 'Those wishing to travel to the regions of Pavers End and beyond can now embark on platform seven. As a special today from the Establishment, all prices will be waived.'

Iris leapt to her feet. Pavers End was *her* home!

She hurried along the corridor, weaving through the refugees, until she reached platform seven. The airship docked there was already accepting passengers. Iris joined the queue, feeling dizzy and elated.

Half an hour later, she was buckled into her seat, exhaling a long deep breath. She would reach home in an hour—a fraction of the time it took to arrive at the mine.

As she settled back in the comfortable leather seat and stared out the window, she noticed a lone star glimmering in the sky and contemplated how miraculous her day had been.

'Thanks for everything, Pender, wherever you are,' she muttered, closing her eyes as the airship rumbled to life.

# *DEAR SOUL CATCHER*

## ANNALIESE HUDSON

My legs were lost beneath the sea of dead butterflies, a veil of fractured wings like shattered stained glass cutting into my skin. It was as if I had stepped into a spider's den, with bleach-white dots painted over withered wings like millions of leering eyes.

A hand lurched forward from the ocean of indigo wings, bruised fingers clutching my wrist like that of a drowning sailor.

'He's coming,' the girl whispered, tears making tracks through the blood on her cheeks.

'Who's coming?'

She pulled me closer, her nails digging into my skin as she looked at me with big white eyes.

'Help me,' she said, before dragging me underneath.

I lunged from the covers of my hospital bed, clutching my throat as I gasped for air. My eyes darted from the vandalised brick walls to the other patients who cursed me in their sleep. I froze once my eyes fell upon the butterflies.

The butterflies sat in-between the eyelets of the old beige curtains or fluttered around the dim light of the lanterns. They wore the same wings as the insects from my nightmare, but at least these butterflies lived.

*It was just a stupid dream*, I thought, but even as I soothed my scrambled mind, I could feel eyes on me, digging into my skin. But those eyes belonged to no butterfly.

A man with silver hair sat in his bed at the other end of the ward. His dark eyes studied me, watching as if he were a scientist and I was a fascinating experiment. I was tempted to curse him for staring—in the hospital a patient waking up screaming was about as rare as a butterfly—but he turned away before I had the chance.

A nurse waddled over. A dozen Palmetto corn snakes made of platinum and chipped gold peeped out from under her flaxen hair, holding bottles filled with golden sap between their fangs. She also held a robotic arm in her hands but unlike her snakes, the arm was made of copper.

'The surgery? What happened?' I asked, my right hand instinctively reaching for my left, but it found nothing. The only thing left was a scarred stump.

'The extraction of the *Butterfly's kiss* was successful.' The nurse reached for the remnants of my shoulder, sliding the copper arm on. 'Of course, you will have to take a dose of Immora every day to prevent further spread of the disease. I would recommend keeping it in a safe place and away from candles to avoid any incidents.'

One of her snakes dropped a vial of golden liquid in my new hand, the metallic gears churning as I flexed my fingers.

I stared at the Immora, its solution smooth but thick like blood. 'I had a nightmare. It was like nothing I've ever dreamed of, and there was this girl.'

The nurse nodded. 'The nightmares are a symptom of Immora, so you'll get them for a few more months. As for the girl, well, *she* was a Soul Catcher.' The nurse's smile faded, and the name sent goosebumps down my neck. 'But you must remember whatever you saw in your dream was just that—a dream.'

I nodded but couldn't find it in myself to meet her eyes. I had heard of the Soul Catcher dreams, nightmares of women with contorted limbs and sagged skin, or ingrown nails and fangs that tore through their cheeks, but the girl from my dream hadn't been a monster … had she?

'Where is my aunt?'

'Dr Clove is at reception, but Theo, I really think you should—'

I struggled from the bed, my robotic arm weighing me down as I slipped out the door, leaving room R4 behind.

It was as if I had stepped into a different world as I walked down the corridor, manoeuvring past nurses rushing past with bloody stretchers and patients holding vomit bags to their lips. Not only that but the hospital stank.

It smelt like brown toxins polluting the air or a fly-infested animal carcass buried six feet under sewage. The bitter smell was best described as death's designer perfume, but at least it was better than the powdery taste of a butterfly's wing caught in between my front teeth that still haunted me from my sleep.

'Theo,' someone muttered from behind me, their voice like distant thunder rolling across the sky. 'What are you doing out of bed?'

A lady with a thin sunburnt face sat behind me. A tight black corset embraced her gaunt figure along with a stained white tunic and monocle. Like the nurse, snakes poured out from beneath the woman's long stark hair. However, unlike the nurse's snakes, these robotic reptiles were made of black titanium with a line of red rubies along their bellies.

'I need to talk to you.'

'Can it wait 'til this afternoon?' Aunt Clove muttered, not looking at me as one of her snakes sorted dirty scrubs, another two screwed a vial of Immora closed and one other held a candle as she flicked through hospital records.

'No, it can't. I had a nightmare after my surgery and—'

'Nightmares are a symptom of Immora. Didn't one of the nurses tell you this?' She stood, giving up on the records to rummage through the chemical cabinet to the right of her desk.

'Yes, she did, and she also told me that in the nightmares, patients see monsters.'

'So?'

'I didn't see a monster Auntie, she was just … a girl.'

Glass scattered across the tile as Auntie's snakes fell limp over her shoulders, falling as if they had been gassed. Only the serpent holding the candle was still viable. Leaning towards the candle, Auntie Clove blew it out to avoid the hazard of flame near exposed Immora.

'What?'

'She was asking me for help. I think she was running from someone.'

Auntie Clove grabbed me by my sleeve, pulling me over to

her side of the reception as she peered over boxes to make sure nobody was eavesdropping.

'Not another soul can know about this, okay? You can't tell anybody,' she said, her hands a little too tight around my wrists.

'Alright I won't, but what does it mean?'

'I've seen this happen before. Some of these monsters are smart and they will paint themselves as victims instead of the malicious monsters that they are—the monsters who created the disease that destroyed your arm and cursed us with mortality. They get to you by infiltrating your dreams, and manipulate you into fighting for a hopeless cause.'

'But she's only a girl, surely she couldn't—'

'She's not a girl, Theo; she's a Soul Catcher.' Auntie Clove sighed, massaging the heads of her snakes. 'You should go back to R4.'

'I told you I don't need to rest.'

'Fine, but if you're not resting, I need you working. The hospital is as busy as it's been all week, and I don't need to be worrying about you doing something reckless on top of that. So go to R4 and get rid of these bloody pests.' She scowled, motioning to a butterfly as it landed on the pile of records. 'They're driving me mad.'

I snatched the butterfly net off the desk before marching back down the corridor. Yeah, soooo busy, and yet she always had time to lecture me.

With the rising sun, room R4 was a labyrinth of moaning patients. I slipped past crowded beds and nurses handing out stale bread as I waved the net through the air.

The butterflies flocked into rooms like these because the

scent of death drove them mad and anyone who had survived the *Butterfly's kiss* was like nectar for the little pests.

The butterflies sat in my net without a fuss as I carried them to the far window. I pulled it open and watched as they flew out into the city. They passed stray cats and hairless rats; strangers with yellow teeth and hunched shoulders; and buildings piled on top of each other.

But a few butterflies were smart. They flew past the tin roofs and the thick murky air, gliding towards a golden palace that sat at the top of a hill. Father Immor's kingdom, but also the Soul Catcher prison.

'Beautiful, aren't they?'

I spun around to face a man who I hadn't realised had been sitting beside me. He didn't look at me though, instead he sat back in his wheelchair, admiring a butterfly as it wandered over his scarred knuckles. It was the same man who had stared at me when I woke up screaming.

'You and I have very different perceptions of beauty,' I muttered as I looked at his patient lanyard. The name 'Arthur Boyd' was scribbled over it.

Mr Boyd laughed, the kind of infuriating laugh a father would use when his son said something stupid.

'How could something be beautiful but take so much from you?' I pointed at his amputated legs, hating myself for getting riled up.

'A disease took my legs as a disease took your arm. The reason the butterflies are here is to help us; it is compassion that drives them, not brutality. They are merely nature's way of warning us of death, but they are not death itself.'

'I don't care if they were here at the request of Father Immor himself, I spent weeks in misery lying on those hospital beds because of the *Butterfly's kiss*. I lost my arm, and I could have lost my life too.'

My shoulders heaved alongside my uneven breaths. Boyd still admired the butterfly balanced on his wrist.

'It's sad how fast a man will turn against something he does not understand,' he said, his inquisitive eyes meeting mine. 'Don't you think?'

The butterfly hovered above the man's head as he grabbed my wrist.

'He's coming,' Boyd said, repeating the words I had spent all morning trying to forget. 'You must help her, Theo, save her before it's too late.'

'How do you know my—'

The door slammed open, and Auntie Clove stood puffing in the doorway. 'Everyone out! He's coming, Father Immor is coming now.'

She dodged panicked patients and nurses as she grabbed my wrist, but before she could drag me out into the corridor, I snuck one last look at Arthur Boyd.

He was still sitting in his wheelchair at the back of the room as if he was deaf to the panic around him. He looked out the window with his hands folded in his lap and the butterfly perched on his shoulder.

The hallway was worse than it had been before. Surgeons kneeled on the floor in bloody scrubs; pregnant women cried as they struggled to lay down; and parents pleaded with their children, begging them to behave.

Auntie Clove yanked me down beside her. She held a protective hand over my head as I pressed my cheek against the grimy floors.

For the first time today, the hallway was quiet. All I could hear were muffled footsteps coming from outside.

The front door screeched, and the footsteps grew louder, booming against the walls 'til they came to a stop. I risked a peek but all I could see was a pair of polished golden boots.

'Oh, I'm honoured but please stand, I'm the guest here,' a voice said, one that could only be described as the voice of a god.

Auntie Clove helped me to my feet. Our movements were hesitant as we gazed at our guests.

In the centre of the hall, surrounded by soldiers dressed in golden armour, was Father Immor. The Father spun his closed umbrella in one hand while the other was hidden in the pocket of his long velvet coat. His kohl eyes and inky hair were visible beneath his black top hat and the waterfall of clockwork gears stitched to the trim. A lit cigar stuck out from between his front teeth as the corners of his mouth turned up, his grin so bright it could make a dying man smile.

'I have come because I wish to speak with Dr Clover Brinley and her nephew, alone.'

My heart shuddered to a stop. He knew, but how? How could I have been so stupid? Of course he knew; he was the great Father Immor after all.

Father Immor held the door open with a smile as we stepped back into R4, his soldiers so close I could feel them breathing down my neck.

'It has come to my attention that your nephew here has received a disturbing dream as a result of his Immora medication.'

'You must be mistaken, Father,' Auntie said, like a patient in denial about a diagnosis.

'Clover,' Father murmured with his hand pressed over his heart. 'I want us to trust each other but lying isn't going to help you.'

Auntie had never looked so scared.

'I'm sorry, Father Immor.' I stepped forward but didn't dare to look him in the eye. 'I let my guard down after my surgery and left my mind susceptible to the Soul Catcher's influence. I'm sorry I failed you.'

There was a long pause, the silence excruciating as I waited for the consequences of my crimes, but none came. Instead, Father Immor kneeled before me, taking one hand of skin and another of metal in his own as if I were the god and he was the boy who needed redemption.

'You did nothing wrong, in fact, I was the one who failed you,' he said with his head bowed. 'I tried my best to protect my people from the Soul Catchers, but I too let my guard down and the monster that follows you in your dreams managed to sneak through the security of my kingdom. Now you are suffering the consequences and I'm afraid you must protect yourself from her manipulation for as many nights as she haunts you.'

'But I don't understand. What do I have to do to get rid of her?'

'She will haunt your dreams as long as she walks free but if you manage to capture her and bring her to me, you'll be liberated from her clutches.'

Capturing a Soul Catcher … how hard could it be? Father

must have read my mind because he gave a solemn nod. 'Don't worry, Theo, she will come to you.'

'How can you be sure?'

'She asked for your help, did she not?'

I nodded.

'Then she will come to you, but when she does you must be strong enough to not fall for her lies.'

The Soul Catcher's tear-stricken face flashed before my eyes, but I pushed it away. I wanted to stay cautious, but trusting Father was like leaning back into a warm bubble bath. All doubts seemed to fade as I listened to his reassuring words, like falling asleep to the sound of a lullaby.

'I won't, I promise.'

His black leather gloves gave my hands one last squeeze. 'I wish you the best of luck. Report to me if you find anything.' He stood, following his guards out of room R4.

Father Immor stepped from the ward and out into the corridor where hundreds of eyes followed him but only one voice spoke, a voice that was not the Father's.

'Dear Soul Catcher, Soul Catcher,

How can it be,

That nobody can see you and yet you're my queen?'

The butterfly flapped its wings in rhythm with every syllable as Boyd stared up to the ceiling, singing the words of an indecorous lullaby.

'Why do you sing that lullaby?' Father Immor glared at the man sitting across the hall, his voice piercing the air like ice.

Boyd sang on, never faltering.

Something sharp lurked behind Father Immor's face then,

a sickly, graphic hatred buried behind his eyes. He lifted his umbrella, the canopy imploding into a sphere of fierce golden light, the long slim staff pointed towards Boyd.

I stepped forward, reaching out for Boyd, but Auntie Clove yanked me back into R4, her snakes coiling around me like rope. I tried to fight back, but she didn't loosen her grip.

'Dear Soul Catcher, Soul Catcher,

Live 'til I see,

Nobody can hear and yet here I—'

A flash rolled across the hallway. As my vision returned, I was forced to see something that made me wish I'd gone blind.

Boyd had been reduced to a corpse, skin grey and sockets empty. It looked like it had been decades since his death. The butterfly lay on the floor, its fractured wings struggling to fly.

'Those who wish to join the Soul Catchers will join the Soul Catchers,' Father Immor said, crushing the butterfly under the heel of his golden boot.

The blanket over his limp body made Boyd look like a ghost, floating across the hallway as the nurse steered his chair back into R4.

I sat within the fortress of boxes that lined the reception desk, the tiles like ice under my palms as I leaned against the yellow glass of the chemical cabinet. Auntie Clove's shadow merged with the night as she climbed over the boxes, collapsing beside me like a worn-out puppet.

'I told you to go to bed.'

'I can't.'

The bags around my aunt's eyes were like smudged ink

on paper skin, her silence louder than anything else in the empty hall.

She thought I was a little boy too frightened to close my eyes, but I wasn't scared of the girl who waited for me in my dreams. Rather I feared how long I was willing to fight against her persuasion, if at all.

'Before Boyd died, he talked to me. He was going on about the beauty of butterflies and he told me how people were too quick to judge something they didn't understand, but I don't think he was talking about the butterflies.'

'For Immor's sake, please don't tell me you believed him.'

'But what if he's right?'

'He's not.'

'Maybe he is. Maybe he knew the truth.'

'The truth means nothing if you're dead.'

'But I'm not dead. Maybe if I could just—'

'Theo,' Auntie Clove said and, when I turned, I was shocked by what I saw. She wiped away tears that trickled down her cheeks, desperate to hide them, but her splintered words gave her away. 'Boyd was a fool who thought his death would mean something, but it didn't. You need to promise me you won't be foolish like him. Just promise me that … please.'

I leaned against her, laying my head in the crook of her neck. 'I promise.'

We sat there until the sun slipped beneath the blanket of shadows that outlined the distant buildings, the candles of passing nurses like stars against the darkness.

An impatient knocking rapped against the front door, interrupting the unusual quiet. It was probably a nurse who had gotten locked out during their cigarette break, or a patient who had strayed from their room.

'Don't worry, I'll get it,' I whispered and Auntie mumbled in return.

I dragged my boots along the floor, rubbing my red eyes as exhaustion loomed over me like a shadow. With every step, the knocking grew louder until I threw the door open and a hand shot forward, scarred fingers wrapping around my wrist.

A girl stood in the doorway, leaning against the frame as she clutched her shoulder, the skin swollen beneath her fingers. Her hair was coarse with mud and her dress hung in tatters. I could tell she was emaciated, like one of the starved kids abandoned in dark alleyways. Her eyes were leaking buckets of moonlight as white tears slipped down her cheeks, washing away the golden blood smudged over her upper lip, blood that looked oddly familiar.

'He's coming,' she said, her voice barely a whisper. 'Help me, Theo, please.'

I pulled the Soul Catcher into my chest as if she were any other patient. Her body shivered against my own as I hung her arm over my shoulders and pressed my hand to her side, warm blood slipping through the cracks in my fingers.

She needed desperate attention; her wounds were too infected for just a bandage and some Immora. I was tempted to yell out—it would only take a matter of seconds before a crowd of nurses would find me and take the girl's weight off my shoulders—but I knew I couldn't, not yet at least.

I needed to take her to R4. It was the only ward in the whole hospital that would be vacant until morning when the mortician would arrive. After that, I didn't know what I would do, but I couldn't focus on that now.

Blood spilled along the tiles as I dragged the Soul Catcher to room R4. Once she was inside, I ran to the reception desk, stuffing Immora into my pockets as I pushed past the wall of boxes.

'Auntie! The Soul Catcher is …' I began, but Auntie Clove was asleep, her snakes limp over her slouched shoulders and her eyes squeezed shut.

I could wake her, but what would she do if she woke to a Soul Catcher in her hospital? She would call Father Immor of course, then what would he do? Would he kill the girl as he had Boyd, or would her death be long and horrific? And if the girl was dead what would happen to me? I would be rewarded for my great service, but I would never know the truth.

*You promised you wouldn't be stupid*, a voice whispered in my head, but I pushed the voice away, turning from Auntie Clove's sleeping figure as I disappeared into R4.

The Soul Catcher sat in the centre of the room, a puddle of golden blood around her as she kneeled in front of Boyd's wheelchair, the skeleton's hand held in her own.

'Dear Soul Catcher, Soul Catcher …' The girl whispered, her eyes squeezed closed as butterflies fluttered down to perch over Boyd's sheet-covered body, their wings flapping in unison as they formed a tight circle like a halo of bellflowers splayed over a casket.

Butterflies were wild creatures that followed nobody's will but nature, and yet as I watched, they seemed transfixed by the girl's voice, as if mesmerised by a siren's song.

'Why are you here, Soul Catcher?' I asked.

'My name's Vivette,' she whispered, the butterflies fluttering away as she stood, 'and I came here because I thought I could find help, and I did.'

She smiled but her words only made it worse.

'Why me? Why did you have to ruin my life? I was fine before you intruded into my dreams and ruined everything.'

The Soul Catcher looked taken aback but I didn't care.

'I didn't choose you.'

'Okay, then why am I the only one who saw you in my dreams and not a monster?'

She stared at me, realisation washing over her face. 'You don't know, of course you don't know.'

She grabbed the vial of Immora from my hands and crushed it in her hands. Broken glass fell onto the tiles. She held out her other palm, now blemished by blood, alongside her right, both doused in golden liquid.

'Do these look similar to you?' she asked, her voice trembling. 'Your precious Immora and my blood, it's the same. And when you and other mortals consume it, you get a glimpse into a Soul Catcher's mind.'

'No,' I whispered, a vile sensation washing over me like a thousand little bugs crawling under my skin. 'No, you're lying. Father Immor would never—'

'Really? Well, what if I told you he tortures us too? He does it so when people look into our thoughts, they see nothing but an abused mind. The only reason you saw differently was because I escaped.'

I couldn't breathe. I had wanted the truth, but not like this. I tried to tell myself she could be lying just as Auntie

Clove and everyone else had said she would, but her hands told a different story.

Vivette's face softened, her intent eyes on me. 'I don't know why fate put us together but ...' She looked back over her shoulder, staring at the corpse beneath the sheet. 'But *he* trusted you—that's why he sacrificed himself.'

'Boyd didn't sacrifice himself. He was killed.'

'No, he made Immor kill him so you and everybody else would see who the real monster is.'

I didn't know what to say. I couldn't process anything with all that racket going on outside. Yelling, slamming doors, marching footsteps ... footsteps ...

Wait.

'You called him.' Vivette stepped away from me like a scared little girl. 'No, no, I can't go back, Theo. Don't make me go back.'

'Vivette, I'm not going to let him take you, okay, but you need to trust me ...'

She hesitated, doubt plaguing her eyes, but then grabbed my proffered hand.

We stepped out into the corridor, our backs to room R4 as we stared at Father Immor and his soldier. Immor shot me a grin and lit his golden cigar.

'Theo! You are excellent, my boy, fighting a Soul Catcher with only your two fists. Maybe I should make you one of my soldiers.'

The idea made me sick. 'Who told you that?'

'Well, my soldier, of course—but it was your Auntie who informed him. She said you were too busy guarding the Soul Catcher to make the call.'

My wide eyes fell on my aunt. She looked back at me, her stiff body pressed against her desk as she stood between Father Immor and me, unsure of which side of the corridor she should stand.

'Now,' Immor cheered, his greedy black eyes on Vivette, 'hand the Soul Catcher over.'

Vivette stood forward. I expected her to scream or maybe run for the door, but instead she squeezed her eyes shut, mumbling that all too familiar lullaby under her breath.

'Dear Soul Catcher, Soul catcher,

Why has it been?

Nobody can hear you and yet you're my queen.'

Immor's smile faded as the floorboards croaked, cracks splintering the old painted walls as a deep rumble coursed through the hospital. Vivette's eyes snapped open, glowing like white opals as she screamed.

'Dear Soul Catcher, Soul Catcher,

live 'til I see,

Nobody can hear you and yet here I sing!'

Every door in the hospital flung open as thousands of butterflies flooded into the corridor. The choir of wings was like churning clockwork, knocking down bottles and tearing through scrubs. Auntie Clove dived under her desk as the soldier threw his shield over Father Immor, but without protection himself, the swarm descended.

They scratched at his eyes and crawled under his sleeves as he stumbled, too distracted by the blood leaking down his cheeks to notice the groaning shelf behind him, hundreds of bottles of Immora shaking as the force of the butterflies caused the shelf to fall. A landslide of gold, wood and glass slammed down onto the tiled floor, crushing the soldier underneath.

Vivette leaned against my shoulder, her body cold as I dragged us forward. The ocean of indigo wings parted as we stepped over broken glass, trying to ignore the soldier's muffled pleas as the butterflies hurtled towards him.

Now nobody, not even Vivette, could control the butterflies as they crowded the soldier like maggots over a week-old corpse, the insects overwhelmed by the stink of blood that polluted the air.

I looked back, expecting to see Father Immor running towards us with his staff in hand. Instead, he kicked the soldier's shield into the river of gold, staring at the writhing man before him with disdain as if I had spoiled his best suit.

'I think Theo has chosen his side.'

'No, he's just confused!' Auntie Clove cried as she pulled herself to her feet, her breathing heavy as her desperate eyes darted from Immor to me. 'Theo, tell him how she's manipulating you!'

Father Immor ignored her and instead took one last puff of his cigar. 'As I said to Boyd, those who wish to join the Soul Catchers will join the Soul Catchers.'

Immor let the cigar slip from his fingers, the little flame vibrant as it lashed its orange tongues up to the ceiling, zipping across the golden river before seeping beneath the glass of the old chemical cabinet.

The blast of the explosion threw me backwards, showering my body in glass. Blood and ash stained my teeth as ribbons of smoke whipped the air. The butterflies weaved in between the flames that danced over the burning soldier's body, his eerie shrieks like a nail through my pounding ears.

Vivette lay on the floor behind me, clutching her arm. She tried to pull herself upright, but she had lost too much blood. I needed to get us out of here, before the building collapsed, before Immor found us and before—

'Theo!' Auntie Clove cried, dropping to her knees with an arm extended through a crack in the wall of flames. 'Come on, Theo, just give me your hand, give me your hand and everything will be okay.'

Her hand shook as she reached out for me, tears and sweat washing away the soot that engulfed her distraught face.

I desperately wanted to grab her hand and let her pull me out of this nightmare, but I couldn't, and she knew it too.

'I'm sorry,' I whispered, unable to look at her as I stood.

Auntie Clove's anguished pleas merged with the dying man's cries as I crawled over to Vivette, pulling her frail arm over my shoulder.

Shattered glass littered the hospital's front steps as I slammed my body against the window, a screeching roar echoing around us as we reached the street. The hospital exploded in a flare of red flames, and fractured wings plummeted from the sky like hail, a sea of dead butterflies around us, their white eyes watching as we left the burning hospital behind us.

# *IN A LEAGUE OF HER OWN*

## JEANETTE O'HAGAN

The study held silence and old grief like an ancient mausoleum. Mira pulled in a breath of air thick with polished wood, aged leather and antique books. Dark flocked wallpaper and timber panelling lined the walls between shelves crammed with ledgers, manuals and thick tomes. Clockwork gadgets and small models of Maedon Enterprises' state-of-the-art steam engines crowded every surface, metal gleaming in the muted gaslight.

Mira rubbed the smooth wooden armrest of her wheeled invalid chair, or go-chair, as she preferred to call it. She half-expected to see Father at the head of the conference table—a brooding energetic presence that sucked up all the attention in a room. Instead, the husk of a lawyer, Mr Watawile, fussed at her father's will.

Mira detested her father's inner sanctum, now more than ever. She'd detested the long evening hours it had stolen of her father's presence. She'd detested the way his gatekeepers would hush her and send her back to the nursery wing so he could dream and invent and build his empire undisturbed. A week ago, they'd buried him after a sudden illness. She blinked back tears.

Cousin Franka, sitting opposite Mira, tapped his silver-topped cane on the parquet floor and avoided her gaze. Of a slim, athletic build, with blue-grey eyes and waves of styled sun-bleached hair, Franka managed to make his mourning attire appear the height of Limarian fashion. Fashions for the tall and elegant that now looked dowdy on her, forever seated in her chair.

At least Mira was alive, unlike her father. She shuddered at the thought of his death.

Her lady companion, Verona, leaned forward. 'Are you cold, Mirabel? A knee rug, perhaps?'

'Please. Don't fuss.' Mira shrugged away the hand on her shoulder. Her legs no longer worked but that didn't make her frail and helpless, as her father had believed.

After she'd returned from finishing school in Tarka and celebrated her seventeenth birthday, Father had welcomed her into the business. For a few brief glorious months, he'd coached her in the intricacies and plans of Maedon Enterprises. Given her responsibilities, a management title.

Father and daughter—a team.

That is, until her accident, her foolish mistake. Father had taken Franka into his confidence, shunting Mirabel off to the logistics department.

She'd hoped to prove herself capable of leading the firm. To win back his respect, if not his affection. Now she never would. Today, at the reading of the will, would Father give his empire to his nephew rather than his daughter?

The golden carriage clock chimed.

Franka rapped the table with a gloved knuckle. 'Watawile, why this delay? Commence reading the will.'

The old lawyer in his immaculate but dated outfit rubbed his drooping moustache and coughed. 'As per Mr Teodor Maedon's instructions, we await the arrival of the third major beneficiary of the will.'

Franka's shaped eyebrows arched. 'Another beneficiary? Who else is there?'

As if in response, the door swung open and a muscular young man entered the room.

Mira gasped. Will? The young mechanic had clearly lost his way. Not dressed in his usual goggles, oil-smeared coveralls and steel-capped boots, but in a ready-made wool suit and polished leather shoes. He brought with him a draught of fresh air.

Franka scowled. 'Verbest, what are you doing here?'

Will ran a tan hand through his dark curls and adjusted his cravat. 'I'm acting as proxy for my father, Dinari Verbest.' He pushed a sealed letter across the polished table.

Watawile picked it up, positioned his half-moon glasses over watery blue eyes and scanned the document. 'It seems in order.'

Will nodded and lowered himself into the fragile Empress chair at the table's foot.

Watawile cleared his throat and read. '"I, Sir Teodor Zander Maedon, being of sound mind and without duress, hereby depose of my worldly goods, the Maker be my witness. One hundred kuzats to each of my household staff ..."' Watawile's dusty voice droned on, '"... The house in Curlew Street and ten thousand kuzats to my dear sister, Suraya Madeon-Severen. My silver duelling pistols, the choice of five horses from my stables and ten thousand kuzats to my excellent nephew, Franka Maedon-Severen. To my chief engineer and good friend Dinari Verbest, his choice from my prized steam-cars and ten thousand kuzats. And to my only daughter, Mirabel Lila Maedon, I bequeath all my remaining personal wealth, my mansions in Kito, Tarka and Kuza, as well as my family estates in Tamra and Silisea."'

Watawile took a long swallow from a chilled glass and looked around the table.

And Maedon Enterprises? Mira's heartbeat slowed. She hardly dared to breathe. Father's life work. Would he entrust her with his legacy? Or give it to Franka, as she feared?

Franka shifted in his seat. 'Don't keep us in suspense.'

'Ahem, "Madeon Enterprises, all its premises, factories, stock, patents, contracts, obligations, goodwill and resources, entire and in full, to my true heir."' Watawile looked over his half-moon glasses at each of them.

'Yes, yes,' Franka muttered.

'"To the person who demonstrates their worth by their determination, initiative and will to win."'

A test. Mira looked up at the same time as Will. Their eyes met then skittered away.

'What?' Franka thumped the table. 'Speak plainly, man, not in damned riddles.'

'If you would sit down, sir, all will be revealed.' Watawile shook out the page and continued to read. '"The heir to my business enterprises shall be the first person present in this room who crosses the threshold of the Maedon Enterprises Boardroom at Kuza."'

Not just a test. A race.

Mira let out her corralled breath. So like Father to set a competition, one in which she was at a disadvantage. Was his ghost chuckling to himself at their stunned reactions?

Franka's mouth gaped and Will stared at Mr Watawile, dark brows arched. Then, in tandem, both young men leapt up and sprinted out the door.

'Miss Maedon.' Mr Watawile closed his folder, inclined his head, and left the room.

Mira settled against the wicker lattice of her go-chair. Would she compete? Of course she would.

She flipped open her father's gold pocket watch. The fastest way to Kuza was by airship and the next Albatross class airship, the M.E. *Nebula*, wouldn't leave until half-past noon.

'Verona, pack some essentials. We'll take the company car to the mooring station.'

\*\*\*

The lifting car shuddered to a stop level with the circular boarding platform of the mooring tower. The open-aired platform sat below the conical mooring pylon for easy access into the airship.

The lift attendant, smartly dressed in Maedon Enterprises' green-and-gold livery, hopped off the tall stool in the corner of the lift and pulled back the folding safety gate. 'Smooth flying, Miss Mira.'

'My thanks, Tanrak.'

Before Verona could assist, Mira spun the go-chair's pull rim and propelled herself onto the platform. A gust of wind tugged at her wide-brimmed travelling hat. She grinned. As much as she hated Father's study, she adored flying.

Thirty-three passengers (she'd looked at the manifest while Verona packed) stood in groups around the circular platform, chatting and sipping from fluted glasses. Others, pressed against the outer railings, marvelled at the sprawling city of Kito and the snow-covered cone of Mount Danger on one side and, on the other, the sleek airship floating like a curious silver whale.

Franka turned from chatting to a mining magnate. 'Cousin Mirabel.' He drew out the syllables. 'Are you here to wish me good fortune against the hapless mechanic?'

She tilted her head up. 'On the contrary, I am here to win.'

'Good one, Mira.' Franka chortled. 'You'd need a miracle to pull that off.'

How dare he mock her! 'I—'

A low-pitched siren sounded. The captain's voice crackled over the loud hailer. 'Attention. Passengers prepare for boarding.'

The loading door lowered from under the nose of the M.E. *Nebula* and extended over the railing to form an enclosed gangplank. Two crew rolled over the lower ramp to form a seamless ascent into the belly of the airship.

'You know, your father never intended for you to lead Maedon Enterprises, even before your accident,' Franka said. 'This contest makes that clear. How can you compete in an invalid chair?'

'It's a go-chair, Franka.' Mira's hand itched to slap his smirking face. Instead, she pressed the lever releasing the chair's clockwork motor and zoomed towards the gangplank.

Franka stumbled backwards. 'I say!'

Mira ascended the enclosed gangplank, only braking

upon reaching the lift. She savoured the stunned look on her cousin's smug face.

But her triumph faded. Franka had to be right. Father hadn't expected her to compete, let alone win.

'I see you've made some modifications to your chair, Miss Maedon.'

Mira startled at Will's soft drawl. He leaned against the mural of the *Nebula*, arms folded, his bronzed face unreadable.

'Will! How did you board before me?'

The side of his mouth quirked. 'I boarded with the crew; one of the advantages of being the son of the chief engineer of Maedon Enterprises.' He cocked his head. 'Is the chair your design? How did you get it to self-propel? Clever.'

'Clockwork.'

His malachite-green eyes widened. 'Difficult. Where do you store the energy?'

'I'm still working on that. Only good for short distances so far.'

Will grinned. 'Still handy to get past nuisances.'

She stiffened. He'd overheard Franka's rant. 'I suppose you also think I'm foolish to compete.'

'Better you than that stuffed shirt.' He pushed off the wall. 'But I promise you, I'm going to win for my father.'

Mira knew how determined Will could be, but she hadn't survived the searing flames of the crash, the months in hospital and rehabilitation, to be beaten by anyone. Not even by Willan Verbest.

***

The faint hum of steam engines and whisper of wind across the canopy formed a comforting backdrop to the *Nebula*'s flight. Mira wheeled her go-chair along the starboard promenade to the sloping glass windows lining the outer skin of the ship.

The jungle sprawled like a verdant quilt beneath them. The branching silver lines of the Uryadi River coiled through the patchwork of greens and occasional splash of purple. A large flock of macaws scattered like sparkling red and green beads. Mira leaned closer to catch the smudge of snow-capped mountains along the western horizon, clouds piling in towers above them like ruffled pillows.

The airship sailed over the bustle of creatures in the vast forest and the people in towns and villages clinging to the river's edge. It felt surreal, floating above the world in a race for the future of her father's company.

Mira spun the chair and zipped along the promenade toward the stern, her gloved fingers spinning the pull rim faster and faster.

'Why in such a hurry, Miss Maedon?'

Mira slowed the chair and glanced through the open arches into the lounge. Will sat in a wicker chair, an open book in his hands and a twinkle lurking in his dark green eyes. Other passengers lounged around the room, writing letters, talking, or reading newspapers.

Will put the book aside, pulled a brass pocket watch from his top pocket and flipped open the case. 'Nineteen hours, eleven minutes and fifty-two seconds since we left Kito, but however fast you move, we will all arrive in Kuza at the same time.'

'Obviously.' Mira tucked a wayward red curl behind her ear and shot him a severe look. Did he think he could slip back into the easy friendship of the past, after leaving to work for a rival firm following her accident? No explanation. No communication. Nothing until this silly contest to win her inheritance.

'Couldn't sleep? Neither could I.' He got up and strolled toward her. 'I thought that prune-faced lady companion never left your side.'

Mira stifled a giggle. Verona took her duties seriously. 'Now Will, be kind. I sent her to … to do something.'

He waved at the back of her go-chair. 'Want an assist?'

Her shoulders tightened. 'I am quite capable, thank you.'

'I don't doubt it. Still, it doesn't hurt to accept help on occasion.'

He moved closer. The familiar scent of sunlight, soap and steam oil invoked the happy years she'd spent with him and his father in the Maedon workshops, tinkering and inventing. A welcome sanctuary, for unlike Father, Mr Dinari had never shut her out.

'For old time's sake?' Will's eyes crinkled with a hopeful smile.

'If you wish.'

'Onwards, then?'

She released the brake and the go-chair glided forward. 'Why are you competing against me, Will? To punish me?' The words flew out before she could catch them back.

The chair hitched a moment before continuing. 'I told you, I'm proxy for my father. He built Maedon Enterprises with his ingenuity, vision and hard work in equal measure with your father's money, drive and ambition.'

'That's not fair. Father did more than bankroll the company.'

'They sparked off each other. Baba deserves to inherit Madeon Enterprises more than Franka-blasted-Severen.'

When they reached the end of the corridor, Will turned her and headed back toward the bow. Silence hung between them, weighted with unspoken words. Mira pinched the folds of her muslin skirt. Father and Dinari Verbest had been partners in all but name. Yet Dinari had always seemed content to leave the control with Father ... 'Maybe more shares—'

'You assume, like your cousin, that common folk like us should not aspire above our proper station.'

The bitterness in Will's words stung. 'You believe I don't deserve to inherit. That I should confine my activities to the drawing room because I can't walk!'

The chair jerked to a sudden stop. 'Not at all. I ...'

She could hear guilt hitch in his voice. 'Don't lie to me, Will. You are just like Father and Franka and everyone else.'

'Mira, you know your way around a spanner and a steam engine better than anyone because my baba taught you.'

'So why don't you think I can lead Maedon Enterprises? Why didn't Father?'

'He took you on when you came back from finishing school.'

'Yes. And after the accident he ignored me.' She propelled the go-chair out of Will's grasp and spun to face him. 'Just like you did. I woke up in hospital and you weren't there.'

Will threw up his hands. 'Mr Maedon blamed me for the crash.'

'I told him it was my idea to test the prototype.' She deflated. 'Will, are you sure this is what your father wants?'

Will's jaw set. 'My father deserves more than some shares in the company he helped to build.'

'And so do I. Is that what you want, to disinherit me?'

'You still have the personal estate. Mira, you can't win this race. Blame your father for this ridiculous contest, not me.'

Her cheeks flamed. 'You are just like the others. You expect me to—'

A flash of movement behind Will's shoulder caught her eye. A man slipped out the door at the end of the promenade, nursing his wrist. A door that led to the inner workings of the airship. Odd.

'Never mind.' With a final glare, Mira wheeled from Will, her view blurred by tears.

\*\*\*

Mira twirled the handle of the silver mirror and fumed. Why did she let Will get under her skin?

'This one would suit.' Verona fastened a lace collar to Mira's vinka-wool dress. Next, she pinned a black feather and lace fascinator on Mira's red-gold curls and clinched the three-stranded pearl necklace around her neck.

Mira glanced at her reflection in the mirror. A bronzed oval face with waif-like grey eyes stared back at her.

'Is something out of place?'

'No, Vee. As always, your ministrations are perfect.'

Mira handed Verona the mirror. She nodded approval at Verona's austere grey silk outfit, quashing a spark of envy at the older woman's waspish waist and perfect posture.

Verona stowed the dressing case away in a recessed cabinet and secured the small, fold-out desk to the wall. Roomier than most, Mira's cabin still made use of every available space.

'Did you check with the communications room? '

'As you requested.' Verona handed Mira a slip of vanilla-yellow paper.

Mira unfolded the telegram and read: *Car will be waiting.* She smiled. She'd leave her competitors fighting the crowds to hire a cab.

'Let's go sample the pre-dinner treats.' She manoeuvred the chair through the curtained door into the corridor.

Strange. The wheels seemed less responsive.

Turning left, she entered the port promenade, the line of angled windows along the side letting in golden afternoon light. Haunting strains of windpipes came from the mahogany gramophone. Passengers sipped cocktails and admired the *Nebula*'s bulbous shadow racing over the dense jungle below.

Through the arches to the dining room, gallery staff laid out gold cutlery and white napkins on small tables. The savoury smell of roast meat and spiced vegetables perfumed the air. Despite her tension, Mira's stomach rumbled.

A silver napkin holder rolled off a table and a server hurried to catch it.

With a soft thud, another napkin holder hit the floor and rolled towards the far wall.

The hairs on the back of Mira's neck tingled. She could feel a subtle pull on her chair toward the stern. Her pulse accelerated.

'Vee, the airship is tilting.'

'Imagination, my dear.' Verona tittered into her fan.

Was she imagining it? No, if anything the feeling of being off-kilter grew stronger. Mira spun her go-chair and headed back to the lifting car.

'Mirabel, wait.' Verona hurried behind her.

Silence ruled on the short trip down and continued as Mira wheeled into the control room. Tall windows offered panoramic views. Crew operated the propulsion controls on port side of the gondola and the lifting controls on the starboard side. Kaptan Nemos and Will conversed on the bridge.

The Kaptan straightened. 'Miss Mira?'

'Kaptan, the *Nebula* is tilting towards the stern.'

The Kaptan gave a sharp nod. 'Yes. We're releasing water ballast from the bow and I've sent some of the crew to the stern to provide extra trim.'

'We will leave you to do your job, Kaptan.' Verona took the handles of the go-chair.

'A moment.' Mira engaged the brake lever. 'And the cause? We have favourable weather.'

Nemos lifted his peaked hat and ran a hand through stiff white hair. 'A few of the stern bladders are leaking helium from what appear to be tiny holes.'

Will's eyebrows crunched together. 'Strange. A defect in manufacturing?'

'More like from a sharp object.' Kaptan Nemos met Mira's eyes. 'We must find the nearest mooring to repair the airship and fully investigate the cause, Miss Mira.'

'Not easy in the jungle,' Will muttered. 'Kuza's the closest mooring tower, close to three hundred lek and several hours away.'

Mira visualised the Maedon network. 'Araya had a mooring tower installed recently. It's an hour away.'

'Good thought.' The kaptan fiddled with his hat. 'We will

need to arrange accommodation for our passengers until we're ready to sail again.'

Mira felt her hope sink like ballast. They'd be stranded in the jungle. 'Yes, of course.'

She looked straight at Will. He returned her stare, his face like granite. He wouldn't wait in comfortable accommodation for *Nebula* to recommence her journey, not even for an hour. Nor would Franka. Nor could she.

\*\*\*

Mira wheeled out of the Araya mooring tower into the cobblestone plaza. Warm air hit her like a wall, redolent with vegetation, river water and crowded humanity. The sun fled, flinging fiery embers across the sky. In the east, the golden and silver orbs of Nardva's two moons floated together above the darkening horizon.

'Mirabel, are you listening?' Verona's voice was brittle with impatience. 'Wait inside while I arrange for a carriage to take us to the hotel.'

'On the contrary, we need transport to Kuza.'

Verona sighed and shifted their carpet bag from one hand to the other. 'How?'

Good question. To the right, the jungle town of Araya lay shrouded by the fast-lengthening shadows, yellow light spilling onto the street from the windows of homes and a packed tavern. A woman with layered skirts and a scarf over her hair ambled along, lighting a few lonely gas lights with a long lighting stick. Across the plaza, mist curled over the dark muscular swirl of the river, a few fishing boats swayed at their moorings, and a small, darkened steamer rested alongside the docks. Boats could sail as far upstream as the White Cascades. From there, she could go by road.

Verona's hand brushed her shoulder. 'You've made a grand effort, Mirabel, but a lady knows when to admit defeat. This place is wild, dangerous, the roads impassable.'

Disgruntled passengers streamed out from behind them towards the waiting horse-drawn carts. The next Maedon steamer, the *River Queen*, wouldn't dock until after sunrise tomorrow.

'Be careful of my wife, sir,' the gravelly voice of an older man called out.

'Hey, watch it!'

A child let out a high-pitched cry.

Mira turned. Franka emerged from the disgorging crowd, swinging his walking cane like a scythe at passengers too slow to get out of his way. He stalked towards the docks, his manservant in his wake.

Oil lamps winked into life on the steamer as though suddenly unshielded. White smoke puffed from the stack into the red-and-purple sky. Almost as if they'd been waiting. Her eyes narrowed. Franka. He would gain a ten-hour advantage.

If she could get there first, maybe she could negotiate her way on board. Mira sent her go-chair jolting over the pavement stones.

'Where are you going?' Verona hurried after her.

Franka looked over his shoulder and sprinted ahead in a loping stride.

'No, you don't.' Mira engaged the clockwork motor and zipped in front. Reaching the docks, she called up to the brawny man standing at the gunwales. 'Friend, can I hire your steamer to go upriver?'

He squinted down at her. 'Any other day, miss. But I already have a hire.'

'Why have one when you could have two? I can pay well.'

'Pardon me, cousin. We don't have room.' Franka pushed past her and jumped aboard the ship, his man scrambling on board after him. The cuff of the man's coat sleeve hitched up, revealing a bandage around his wrist.

'Ready to cast off, Kaptan?'

'Aye, sir.'

A piercing whistle split Mira's eardrums as the steamer pulled away and headed upstream, against the flow of the river.

\*\*\*

'Slide it, he has a boat ready and waiting.'

Mira's heart slammed against her ribs. 'Will!' She turned her neck and glared at him. He wore an open-necked shirt with multiple pockets, a leather jacket and sturdy boots. A leather satchel hung over his shoulder.

'Miss Mira.' Will nodded at her. 'Severen is quick on his feet, I grant him that.'

'He'd already arranged the steamer.' How? Anger broiled through her. Franka's valet had an injured wrist and was same build as the man emerging from the restricted area. 'Franka sabotaged the *Nebula* to force the early landing.'

'What a silly suggestion,' Verona spluttered. 'Come on, the carriage is about to leave.'

'If so, he put everyone's life at risk.' Will hitched his satchel higher. 'Look, I'm off to hire a boat. I can walk you to the carriage.'

'We are not defenceless. Verona has a pistol and I have my chair.'

'As you wish. I learned long ago—never argue with a Maedon.' Will dipped his head and strode towards the town.

In the west, the glow faded from the sky. A lonely gas lamp at the docks cast a circle of faded light. The mournful cry of an owl drifted across the dark water.

'We could hire a boat.' Mira scanned the shrouded fishing boats. The *River Queen* would be faster, but even an old sailboat could go a long way in half a day.

'I am not going on one of those death traps.' Verona put down the carpet bag and folded her arms. 'Nor sleeping overnight at the docks.'

Mira's shoulders slumped. Fatigue, her aching back and a sudden twist of hunger claimed her attention.

*Whoo. Whoo. Whoo.*

The wailing blast of a steam horn sounded from around the riverbend, too full-throated to be Franka's hire. Had she miscalculated the *River Queen*'s schedule?

She slapped her forehead. Maker's grace, a smaller firm had started a service on the Uryadi River during Father's sudden illness. She blinked back a wave of sadness. She had to get on that steamer.

'Will, wait up.' Mira wheeled the chair after him.

He didn't slow.

She engaged the clockwork motor. Her go-chair caught Will moments before the motor ran out. 'Will, listen. I have a plan.'

'You don't give up, do you? Remember the last time you ignored my advice?'

She shuddered at the memory of the ground rushing towards her, the bone-breaking jolt, the smell of scorching wood, the searing pain of burning flesh. 'Willan Verbest, are you blaming me for what happened?'

He swung around, face anguished. 'No, I blame myself. I should have stopped you. Why do you think I left?'

Her whole body vibrated. 'Because Father blamed you. Because …' Her voice caught on unshed tears. 'Because you couldn't bear seeing me, damaged, broken. Because you are just like everyone else, wanting to hide me away like a cracked porcelain ornament shoved to the back of the cupboard.'

'No—'

'We don't have time for this. Listen to me. A Venturan Co Steamer is about to leave from the other dock.'

'How can you know that?'

'Apart from being shunted off to work in logistics? I heard the boarding whistle. We've got ten minutes, if that, and the other dock is five lek upstream.'

'You are a genius.' Will flashed a grin at her. 'Five lek in ten minutes—we need transport. Wait here, I'll be back.' He rushed down the street.

A brisk wind picked up from the river, swirling and dispersing the mist, sending chill bumps skittering across her arms.

'Doubt that young man is coming back.' Verona sniffed.

Franka would abandon her without a moment's thought. Would Will? He had changed since the accident. Was that because of his guilt, not the disgust she'd imagined?

A soft *clop*, *clop* echoed from the dark and an old cart pulled by a bony horse emerged into the pool of gaslight. Will jumped down from the box. 'Here, let me help you up.' He unbuckled the straps holding her in the chair, scooped her up, and placed her on the hard wooden seat. He helped Verona up and then secured Mira's go-chair in the back.

Excitement fizzed through her. Will came through for her. She released the brake, slapped the reins and urged the cart horse into a shambling gallop.

They were back in the race.

***

Mira wheeled into the communication room on the S.S. *Tramp* and handed the messages to the young lad on duty with two copper pina. 'Can you send this at once?'

The lanky fellow gave her a lopsided grin. 'Too right, miss.'

She smiled and headed out onto the deck. By the time the *Tramp* reached White Cascades, Samsen would be waiting with her steam car. Franka wasn't the only one with resources.

Grey smoke from the steamer's stack drifted over the swirling, emerald-green water. Dense walls of vegetation crowded either side of the river. A flock of snow-white parrots rose like confetti in the pale dawn sky.

Ahead, a smaller steamer chugged against the current in a cloud of dark smoke. Franka's steamer. It swerved as though to block their passage, but the *Tramp* continued undaunted.

A tall, slim figure in top hat and tailored grey coat stood beside the brawny kaptan in oil-stained coveralls. Mira cupped her mouth and called across the water. 'Beautiful morning, cousin.'

'Decorum, Mirabel,' Verona murmured.

'The race isn't over yet, Mirabel,' Franka called back. 'If you concede now, I'll give you a sixth share in the company.'

'Ha!' Will emerged from the engine room, wiping his hands on a cloth. 'Don't trust him. Not after the stunt he pulled on the *Nebula*.'

'What rubbish you are talking about, Verbest? Don't trust this ruffian, Mira.'

'The guardia will be waiting for you at White Cascades with some pertinent questions,' Mira shot back.

'A mere nuisance. You will regret turning me down when I win.' Franka smirked.

The *Tramp* slid past the smaller steamer, leaving Franka in its wake.

***

A couple of hours later, S.S. *Tramp* approached White Cascades village. Just five lek downstream the river descended a narrow gorge from the high plateau in a stretch of foaming, turbulent water. The morning sun radiated heat like a torch and Mira mopped her face with a white kerchief.

The steamer edged close to the docks and blew its whistle. Sailors rushed to throw ropes down to the dock workers, who secured them to the bollards.

Her beautiful yellow vehicle, Bessi, sat waiting with Samsen at the wheel.

'Come, Verona.' Mira directed her go-chair down the ramp.

Samsen jumped out of the car, undid the straps and lifted her into the driver's side. Verona climbed in and settled beside Mira.

Bessi purred like a satisfied cat. 'Ready?' Mira asked.

'Yes, Miss Mira. Water vented from the condenser and the furnace lit.' Samsen stowed the carpet bag and her go-chair in the custom-designed storage compartment. He jumped up behind.

Mira glanced at the temperature and pressure gauges, watching the needles climb. She pulled on her goggles and leather gloves. 'Let's go.'

'I thought you would never ask.'

Mira whipped her head around at Will's voice. He looked natty with googles and a travelling scarf beneath his leather jacket. How did he keep sneaking up on her?

He touched his cap and pulled up to sit beside Verona.

Mira scowled at him. 'Samsen, please remove this gentleman.'

'I'll leave if you ask me.' Will raised his dark eyebrows. 'But fair's fair. I got you to the steamer.'

She did owe him, but if they both arrived at the Kusa M.E. office, her chance of being first to the boardroom greatly diminished. If she wanted to win, she needed to be ruthless, uncompromising, determined.

But, Maker's grace, was that the person she wanted to be?

Mira growled, 'Stay then.'

She released the brake and hit full throttle.

\*\*\*

More than two hours later, Mira drove through the streets of

Kuza, passing the golden domes of the Old Palace. The city formed the bottom of a shallow bowl rimmed with snowcapped mountains, the tall office buildings and the houses of the rich clustering in the centre. Maedon Enterprises Head Office, however, was closer to the edge in the Koraktil Quarter. The tricky bit would be getting down from Bessi and into her chair in the shortest time possible.

Mira drove around the fountain, avoiding the market stalls around the plaza, and headed beneath the arch into the wide street. Crisp air slapped her cheeks. She slowed as she approached the towering stone building with 'Maedon Enterprises' emblazoned on the outside.

Will launched out of his seat and onto the street before the steam car had fully stopped.

'Samsen, the go-chair.' Mira pulled on the brake.

The lad scrambled to release the go-chair and set it on the pavement.

Mira unbuckled the straps holding her in the seat. 'Verona, a hand.'

No answer.

Mira looked up and gasped. Will ran up the flight of steps to the entrance of Maedon Tower and Verona sprinted close behind, one hand clamped on her hat, the other lifting her dress's hem.

'Here, Miss Mira.' Samsen lifted her and placed her into the chair. 'Don't worry about Bessi, I'll see she's looked after.'

Mira pulled herself together and released the go-chair's brake, speeding towards the ramp adjacent to the stairs. At the top, the porter opened the doors and bowed her into a large atrium. Light streamed through the domed roof onto the malachite-green and cream tiles. Ignoring greetings, she headed toward the dual lifts at the end of reception.

Will jabbed the lift button, then glanced towards the door to the stairs, no doubt calculating whether running up ten flights of stairs would be quicker than waiting. Not an option Mira could consider.

'Verona, wait up,' Mira called.

'If Will can stand in proxy for his father, then I can also be a proxy,' Verona puffed. She reached the lift as it arrived with a ding.

Verona could stand in for her. That evened her odds of winning, but it wouldn't feel the same as having won herself. She pushed harder, her shoulders aching, her heart tapping out an urgent rhythm.

The lift attendant folded the latticed safety gate. Will and Verona piled into the lifting car.

'Tenth floor,' Will shouted.

'Hold the lift for me, Sylvi,' Mira called.

'Yes, Miss Mira,' The young woman stared at the three of them, questions written large on her face.

Just three strokes more.

'For heaven's sake,' Verona snapped and pushed the young woman aside and yanked the safety gate with such force it hit the opposite wall with a loud crash. A clang and a whirl of the motor, and the lifting car trundled upwards out of sight.

Too late.

But there was another lift. She wheeled towards it, jabbing the button.

*Please, please, please.*

Fifteen precious seconds later, the second lift arrived.

'Miss Mira.'

'The board room, Kimsak.' Mira pushed a strand of hair from her sweaty face and rolled into the lift car.

The ascent felt agonisingly slow. Mira stared at the silk carpet, the floral wallpaper, the gleaming gasalier and the large gilt-edged mirror reflecting a dishevelled redhead with large grey eyes in a cane chair on wheels. What had made her think she could do this? Would it be so bad if Will won? He and his father would keep the spirit of the company, based on innovation, adventure and the vision of improving the common people's lives. Better than Cousin Franka could. But no, she had come this far. She wasn't going to give up.

Her stomach flew upwards as the lift jolted to a stop.

Kimsak pulled the gate open and Mira rolled into the long, dim corridor leading to the boardroom. Ahead, Will ran like a deer, Verona puffing several paces behind.

Mira engaged the clockwork motor, praying it would be enough to make up the distance. She zipped by portraits of past Maedons parading down the wall, their eyes following her progress.

She'd almost caught up with Verona, but Will was way ahead. Within a pace of the solid carved door, he reached out, touching the polished gold knob.

Verona pulled an object out of her pocket, something sleek and metallic with a mother-of-pearl handle. Something cold and deadly. A pistol.

Verona thumbed off the safety, cocked the trigger and straightened her arm. She intended to fire—at Will.

'No!' Mira's heart thundered in her ears. 'Will, watch out!' She swerved the chair, crashing into Verona. The chair toppled, sending Mira flying.

A bang ballooned out, popping Mira's ears and shaking the framed paintings on the wall. The stink of hot gunpowder singed her nostrils.

'No!' *Please, please, don't let Will be hurt.*

The large, spoked wheels of the go-chair spun crazily above her, and her head hurt. Somewhere in the distance, an alarm bell rang. Someone was screaming and it wasn't her.

She struggled to sit up, pushing against a large, soft mass.

Verona. The woman had cushioned her fall. Her right arm hung at a strange angle and blood dripped into her pale eyes. She clutched Mira's arm and subsided into sobs. 'It hurts.'

No doubt it did, but what about Will? Her heart clenched. Had Verona killed him?

Unstrapping her legs, Mira pulled herself by her elbows over Verona, wriggled to sit up against the wall and looked down the corridor.

Will stood blinking at a dark, smoking hole in the door, level with his head. A line of blood leaked down his temple. He stared at Verona, pale beneath his tan skin. 'She tried to kill me.'

Mira rounded on Verona. 'I would never want to win on such terms!'

Verona's face twisted into a snarl. 'Do you think I did this for you? A spoilt brat who has had everything handed to her on a silver platter?'

Mira flinched as if Verona had thrown cold water in her face. 'Then who?' Mira slapped her forehead and winced. Verona could be proxy for only one other person. 'Franka. No wonder you kept urging me to give up. What did he promise you?'

'He gave his word he would marry me if I helped him win. I wasn't shooting to kill. Just to …'

'Could have fooled me, Miss Verona Arnica.' Will stalked down the corridor towards them. 'Without Mira's warning, I'd have a date with the morgue about now.'

'Will, get inside.'

He knelt beside her. 'Are you hurt?'

'No, not much. But the race isn't over. Franka might still be out there.' She pushed up against the wall and grabbed hold of her go-chair.

'You saved my life.' Will righted the chair. 'I'd still be on the river without you.' He scooped her up, his strong arms around her, the scent of soap and engine oil enveloping her.

'True, but I would still be halfway up the river on the *River Queen* if you hadn't fetched that horse and cart.'

He settled her into the chair. 'And without your steam-car, I'd be still on the road. You not only know the business inside-out, you have your father's inventive genius.' He nodded at her chair. 'And his determination and courage. You deserve to win. Go for it, Miss Maedon. I'll watch her.' He pointed his chin at Verona.

'We make a good team.' She caught hold of his hand. 'The terms say whoever arrives first gets the company.'

'Yes, and I'd rather it be you if only one of us can win.'

She laced her slim fingers between his strong ones. 'What if we arrive at the same moment?'

A slow smile spread across his face. 'Partners?'

'Equal partners.'

'What about me? I could be badly injured,' Verona screeched. 'My arm.'

The lift dinged. Mira glanced down the corridor. Franka jumped out.

Mira released Will's hand. 'Let's go.'

She wheeled the go-chair down the corridor, Will keeping pace beside her. Mira nodded at the large portrait of Zander Maedon, founder of their house, above the boardroom door. He seemed to smile down at her and welcome her in to claim her inheritance.

# RUN

## SHAYE WARDROP

*Run*, I tell myself. *Run.*

My tattered boots slam into the grass-covered concrete and I pray for level ground, even though I know how cracked the streets have become from plants pushing through in search of the sun. It feels like I've swallowed glass instead of the sticky brown ration loaf I ate this morning, but I keep going. Keep pushing.

The scavenger dogs shouldn't be out this far. They usually stick to the inner city where the rats and snakes thrive. Yet here they are. And they're hungry.

I sprint down Green Street and onto Lush, with its mammoth broken houses that seem bigger than any family could ever need—much bigger than my simple hut. Most of the street signs have either fallen, broken or disappeared now, but the collectors have maps of the city from before the Primes took the world, and they re-named the streets so they could assign us salvagers areas to search for things for the Crow's collection. Green and Lush are on my list.

A deep, guttural sound rumbles behind me—the sound of feral hunger. I don't look back, but I imagine drooling mouths flinging splashes of disease-infested goop on the road. I think of rotten fangs cracking bones, and memories of every half-eaten animal I've ever come across flash in my head.

Old Jome says dogs were human companions before the Crow and the other Primes invaded, but it's hard to believe the unrelenting beasts behind me are descendants of the fluffy creatures Jome describes.

*Run, Miram*, I tell myself. *Run faster.*

I rush past Old Yellow, sitting half on the road and half on the concrete in front of the biggest house on Lush like it was abandoned in a hurry. I've passed the rusting yellow car a hundred times while salvaging from this area, but I've never once wished it worked. Not that it would matter if it did. I've only heard stories about how to drive a car and the Crow would come for me if I even turned it on. Running from scav dogs is no excuse for using power. The Crow has always been clear about the rules of our territory. *No harm to the land, no power, no plastic, no old-time ways.*

A scav howls behind me and this time I turn, eager to check the distance between us. I wish I hadn't. It's smaller. The scavs have more stamina than me and they'll use it to wear me out. I need somewhere to hide, but all the houses on Lush are too easy to get into. They have no doors or windows anymore, and the scavs will just follow me in.

My stomach cramps and my legs feel like they're on fire, but it's run or die at this point.

I turn off Lush and race into a shopping district—places

people used to buy things and eat food, I've been told. I haven't explored the area before—it's not on my list—but the buildings here are taller than the houses I'm used to. Everything is big, squarish and flat; harder for the scavs to get into, I would think, so I run down the crumbling road.

Straight into Grace.

'What are you doing here?' I grab her arm and keep running. 'I've got scavs on my tail.'

'I know,' says Grace. 'Toby told me. He saw you running.'

'That doesn't mean you come here.'

'I wanted to help.'

I don't say anything and keep running, pulling Grace and scanning the silent buildings as I go. I need an open door. I need to know we can get in so we can find somewhere safe to hide. But I also need to know I can keep the scavs out. And now, I have to do it dragging my foolish younger sister with me.

'Miram, over here.'

It's Toby. He's standing in the doorway to a grey building covered in strangled vines. It's pretty smashed up and the door is missing, but he's waving frantically. 'In here,' he calls again.

'No door,' I yell.

'It's safe.'

I haven't trusted Toby and his brothers since I caught them lying about food rations to get more than their share, but what choice do I have? The scavs are howling again, calling more to the chase now that their expected meal has just got bigger.

I yank Grace behind me, and we cross the road to the doorway. Toby's already inside, sprinting up a staircase two steps at a time. We follow, and he slams a door behind us at the top.

But it's falling off its hinges and I doubt it will hold the scavs for long. If this is Toby's master plan, we're done for. But he's running down the hall, so there must be more places to hide further in.

It's dark and wet in the hallway. The walls are warped and they smell like damp soil; water damage from a leaking roof most likely, which makes me nervous. And not just because it means the scavs might find a way in. Buildings fall all the time these days. Eighty years of neglect will do that.

Toby heads into a room filled with rotting wooden tables. They're all over the place, upside down and piled up on the side. There's a door at the back and Toby pulls a key from his pocket.

My throat feels dry. 'Why do you have that key?'

'Just get in the room, Miram.' He unlocks the door.

'You can't have that key, Toby. If the Crow finds out …'

'Get in the room, Miram. Unless you'd like to stay out here and play with the scavs.'

I can hear them. They're coming up the stairs.

Toby pushes Grace into the room and steps inside.

'Miram, please,' begs Grace.

This is not how I saw my escape from the scavs turning out. This is not where I want to be.

I step through the door and Toby slams it behind me.

\*\*\*

It's pitch-black inside. No windows. A good sign. But I don't like the dark.

A soft hand clutches mine and I squeeze my half-sister's fingers, though I'm still furious at her for coming into the city.

But Grace hates the dark even more than I do, and she'll have trouble breathing if she works herself up too much. That's the last thing we need.

'What's the plan?' I say into the dark. 'Hang out here for the rest of our lives?'

Toby's shuffling around, but he doesn't respond.

'You've obviously been here before,' I say, referring to the key. 'I'm guessing you know this place is secure? But we're trapped in here. You get that, right? If the scavs think we're worth the wait, they won't leave until we come out or they'll find a way in.' There isn't a lot that makes the scavs give up. That's why it's best to stay clear of them altogether.

More banging sounds from somewhere in the dark, and then an orange flickering light fills the room. Toby appears behind it, holding a match as he lights a rusty lantern. The glass is all smashed up, but it still does the job. It casts dancing shadows across the room, and I see what Toby's been hiding.

We're in some kind of storeroom. It's long and narrow, and the walls are lined with shelves of ... stuff. Through the shifting light, I can make out glass bottles, knives, torches, books and various plastic containers—all things we're meant to hand over to the Crow.

I stare at Toby in shock. 'What's wrong with you? The Crow will hang you for this. Where did all this come from?'

But I already know the answer. Toby and his daft brothers have been saving things instead of handing them in and they've been stashing it all here. Stupid, stupid, stupid. We're allowed one item per month from an approved list, and the Crow always knows when we have things we shouldn't in camp. It stares at you with its giant bird eyes, and it just knows things. I've heard all the Primes do it.

Some people think they're psychic—psychic aliens from another planet, getting things ready for more of their kind. Others say they come from old-time scientists tinkering with genetics to create mega-sized intelligent animals.

Jome believes they're spirits of the land come to punish us for nearly destroying it. He says they're taking it all back because humans don't deserve it anymore.

But, really, what does it matter what the Primes are? They're here now. The Crow is here, and it controls us.

A snuffling, growling sound snakes under the door, reminding us of the real reason we're in the small room.

'They'll find a way in,' I say, wishing it wasn't true, but knowing it is.

Toby slips into the plastic chair at the end of the room. 'There isn't one.'

He's so full of himself.

Grace moves further in, away from the scratching scavs. I watch her scan the shelves in the flickering light, looking at things she's never seen before.

'Hey, Miram. Don't you have one of these?' She holds up a green metal pen the colour of the moss-covered rocks by the river.

It does look like my pen, but *my* pen is beneath my mattress—tucked away in the small wooden box my mother gave me the day she left the territory.

My heart pounds in my ears, and I step towards my sister, but Toby jumps up and snatches the pen from her hand before I can reach it.

'Hey,' I say. 'She's just looking.'

'She can look with her eyes.' He slouches back into his chair and crosses his arms around the pen.

Fury bubbles inside me. The Thomas brothers are jerks, but this is something more. 'Where'd you get the pen, Toby?'

'Found it.'

'Where?'

'Around.'

I stand in front of him, staring down, and I can tell he doesn't like it. 'Let me see it.'

'Get your own pen.' He stands to meet my eyes, so close our noses are almost touching. His breath is rank, but I hold still before reaching down and snatching the pen from his hand.

'Hey!' He tries to snatch it back, but it's too late.

I untwist the metal barrel and pull out the letter my mother hid inside. 'Found it, huh?'

He shrugs with a giant smirk on his face.

'Why do you have this, Toby? Did you read it?' I feel like screaming. The stupid pen and letter are all I have left from my mother—her last words before she made a deal with the Crow to be traded into Crocus territory. It's all I have to make sense of the reasons she left me. It means nothing to the Thomas brothers and everything to me.

'Tell me why, Toby,' I say again, but then I get it. 'You're going to try and pin this whole place on me, aren't you? I'm your backup plan if you get caught.'

Toby grins and my jaw tightens. 'You're going to say it's all mine.' The letter is addressed to me. Lots of people have seen me with the useless pen. They know it belonged to my mother. 'Why did you bring me here, Toby? What exactly are you planning?'

My stomach churns. In a world where few people survived the Prime invasion and those of us left are forced to serve them and obey their rules, how can anyone think of betraying their own people?

But Toby does. His brothers do. We share the same hardships and the same enemies, but they have no problem using me to protect themselves.

Maybe Jome is right. Maybe humans don't deserve to rule the planet anymore.

The ceiling crunches above, pulling me back to the now. I squeeze the pen, letting the chill of the metal calm my mind. Toby's betrayal isn't the biggest problem I have to deal with right now, and I need to stay focused. 'Grace, find a weapon.'

I shove the pen in my pocket and we scan Toby's collection. There are knives in a box, but I don't want to get that close to a scav if I can help it. There are old machines, but they aren't helpful.

There!

A shovel is leaning in the corner of the storeroom. I run over and grab it, checking it won't fall apart with the first swing.

Grace has a broom, but the fear in her eyes says she has no idea how she's going to use it, so I thrust the shovel in her hand and take the poorer of the options. The smooth plastic feels slippery and weak, but it will have to do. 'Aim for their heads.'

The banging above us gets louder and I lean my ear against the storeroom door. I can't hear anything out there, but there has to be at least a couple of scavs keeping guard.

'The only way to do this is to run,' I say to Grace. 'Take them by surprise and keep running.'

'Are you insane?' Toby says. 'That's a stupid plan.' He rummages in his knife box and pulls out the longest one he can find.

'You're welcome to stay here and wait for them to drop.' I point to where the ceiling is bulging down in several sections.

Toby grunts. 'You're going to get us killed.'

'Get ready,' I say, and I turn the handle. But the door is suddenly yanked backwards, and I stare into the ugly faces of Marcus and Ruben Thomas.

Marcus is smiling, like he's proud of a secret he knows and I don't. Except I do know.

But we don't have time for that now.

I push past the boys and look around. Three dead scavs lie on the floor, their week-old meat smell wafting around the small space. Marcus passes the blood-stained tree branch in his hand to Ruben and loads a slingshot with a large rock. But it's not going to be enough. There's too many of them.

I turn to Grace. 'Run.'

We sprint through the room and out into the hall. The Thomas brothers laugh as they run behind us, but they shut up when a loud crash echoes from the storeroom.

We have minutes. Seconds.

We leap down the stairs and dash out onto the street. The light is fading, but we run onto the broken road that snakes through the buildings. It feels like a trap. There's nowhere to go but forwards.

The scavs are growling, snapping at Marcus's heels as he runs behind Grace and me. Marcus is shooting at the dogs as he runs, but he isn't doing a great job of hitting them. He loads again, turns and aims, but the dogs go left, disappearing down a small gap between buildings.

I stop, and Grace freezes beside me. Something isn't right. Scavs don't just give up.

The ground shifts beneath me and a shudder vibrates up my legs and through my chest. I know why the dogs have fled.

The boys stop too. They also know what the rumbling means.

The Crow.

Bile fills my mouth, but I start running again—down the crumbling street, over fallen poles and through waist-high grass thrusting through cracks in the road.

The Crow doesn't come into the city that often, preferring to stalk the hills that mark the perimeter of the territory. Why today? Why now?

The street comes to an end, but another one crosses its path, and I recognise the building in front of us. The collection hub isn't far. The brothers pull ahead, and I grab Grace's hand, willing her to be faster.

Then we turn the corner and none of it matters.

Terror and awe pulse through me. The biggest of all the Primes, the Crow stands as tall as a two-storey house. Its sleek black feathers are longer than me. Its claws are as big as the hacker blades we use to clear the fields. Probably sharper, too. There's no point running now.

It lowers its head and its giant yellow eyes—the size of so many broken clocks I've seen in the hallways of forgotten homes—stare at the Thomas brothers.

Toby is closest to me, visibly shaking, a glimmer of green poking out of his fist. What the ... I check my pocket, but it's empty.

The Crow moves its eyes along the line of boys to Ruben.

He's only slightly older than Grace and he'll break the easiest. The Crow knows it.

'Speak.' The Crow's deep voice booms through the streets, leaving a ringing in my ears.

Ruben's chin wobbles, but Marcus taps his arm with the back of his hand to urge him on.

'Sca … scav dogs,' says Ruben. He stares at the ground, too afraid to look the Crow in its giant eyes. 'We ran.'

The Crow hops sideways, sending rocks and gravel flying at our feet. It moves its head in next to me, bringing one eye level with mine.

'Scav dogs.' I agree with Ruben because it's the truth.

It sees the broom in my hand and my stomach drops. Does it already know where I got it? Would it blame me for even being in Toby's storeroom? Should I blurt out the truth to save myself?

Panic bubbles inside me, but the Crow turns back to the brothers, this time to Toby, and he drops my pen on the road.

Toby's eyes widen, his attention fully fixed on the Crow. He knows as much about the Primes as I do. Neither of us knows what it's going to do.

My legs itch to move, itch to escape.

The Crow's hot breath slides from its beak, flows over Toby and hits me in the face. It's thinking. Judging. Deciding.

'Run,' says the Crow. 'Run.'

# WHAT AUNT MAUD ACHIEVED

## JENNIFER HORN

A lifetime of living in the grimy city below had made Dulcie rather immune to the belching smog which now ensconced her cable car as it rattled up the ravine. Through the fumes, she caught glimpses of crude factories and tenements stacked atop each other and wrought-iron bridges curlicuing throughout the heaving metropolis. She gripped the satchel bag with her writing journal inside and tried for all her life to look nonchalant and confident.

As usual, horrifyingly to Dulcie, there were others in the carriage today—five adults in total. She wanted to challenge herself by smiling at them, asking them where they were bound, and perhaps complimenting one of the formidable hats the ladies were wearing. But she couldn't quite meet anyone's eyes and the thought of what to say made her break out into a sweat. It was already hot enough in her bustle skirts and high-neck chemise. She imagined the other passengers looking at her surreptitiously, watching her writhing in her struggle, effortlessly achieving such small social exchanges themselves.

So she stayed silent, making herself smaller against the side of the cable car, and gazed back out at the fabulous view. They had risen above the smog belly and were now audience to the stunning pink-purple hues of the sky. It was common knowledge that such a colour was only because of all the pollution hanging in the air, but she couldn't help but admire it anyway.

Dulcie surreptitiously reached for her journal to do what she always did when this horrible tension surfaced. And it had turned out she was quite good at it—penning her anguish into poetry so much that her anonymous works were published regularly in the local gazette. As long as no one deduced it was her, she was glad of this secret achievement. But more importantly, as she let the nib glide over the smooth parchment page, she could already feel the calmness her writing seemed to give.

The sun climbed among the sky's pink hues as the cable car stuttered to a stop at the lip of the ravine. Dulcie watched the shoes of her fellow passengers as their owners disembarked. She picked her way down the familiar streets, lined with squat buildings that were huddled against the constant wind sweeping up from the ravine's edge.

She came to a crooked little tenement at the end of the cul-de-sac and knocked stiffly on its door. The telegram sat crumpled in her satchel, but she didn't need to retrieve it to recall the curious message her brilliant Aunt Maud had sent.

As far as Dulcie could remember, her aunt had always been haphazard in her appearance and work-quarters. However, in recent years, Aunt Maud's compulsive small behaviours had descended beyond merely troublesome. For instance, Dulcie knew that her aunt crossed the flagstone floor, taking great care not to step on the cracks in between. And that she unlocked the door fastenings from top to bottom and turned the last one twice. '*For good measure,*' Maud usually said, not fooling either of them. Her compulsions were the reason she rarely ventured outside these days. Dulcie sometimes dreaded that she saw her own future in her aunt's reclusion.

There was the expected spatter of clicks and mutterings from the other side of the door before it scraped open to reveal a dishevelled woman wearing a utility apron, her grey hair escaping from her updo in lightning-bolt wisps. Recognising her niece, she blinked through her self-prescribed equipment goggles and smiled, reminding Dulcie of an insect.

'Dulcie, darling! So glad you got my telegram,' she gushed, waving Dulcie inside and then enveloping her in arms with stain-blotched sleeves.

'Yes, I was quite alarmed. It almost sounded like an emergency.'

'Not an emergency, dear, but some very exciting developments I just couldn't wait to share with you, favourite relative and all. I sent it as soon as the lovely people from the asylum left. By the way, *loved* your piece in last Friday's paper—*such* a way with adverbials, my dear.'

Dulcie smiled humbly and sat down on one of the threadbare chairs. The weight of her aunt's last remark started to dawn on her.

'You've been experimenting on mad people?'

'Well that's the thing, Dulcie. They're not mad. Besides, they were begging for me to give them a taste of this. They're on the further end of a spectrum of what I'd call cranial sanity.

And Dulcie dear, this is what I've found—the thing is, we *all* are. Why do you think every man holds his head bowed in the streets, lost in the fog of his thoughts? Why every woman worth her salt has been treated for hysteria at some point? It's a wonderful thing, this Industrial Age, but I'm afraid it's wreaking havoc on our neurology.' She turned and said pointedly, 'Even you, my dear girl, and that terrible asylum chapter—all related.'

Dulcie shifted in her seat. She loved her aunt, but why did dear Maud have to revisit her hysteria-afflicted chapter for the sake of scientific curiosity again and again?

'Here, let me explain.' Aunt Maud scuttled over to the foggy chalkboard and tapped out a diagram.

'See, this is the brain, and *here* is the amygdala.' She scratched a circle around it. 'Now if we're able to pinpoint this connection …' Aunt Maud's hand flew across the board as she explained her theory and experiments on this cranial sanity. Dulcie was lost within seconds but found herself nodding anyway.

'Now, Dulcie,' her aunt said, turning from the board. 'If we can do that, the person can still function but without the *burden* of this area going haywire and causing such distress. And thus,' she planted the chalk back on the desk, 'this is how one can become *better*.'

Dulcie must have looked more dubious than she meant to because Maud gave the blackboard a disapproving frown.

'Anyway, I wanted to show you this.' Aunt Maud clapped her hands and took a purposeful step forward. Dulcie felt the beginnings of an anti-climactic wave until she looked down and saw her aunt's boot resting over a crack between the flagstones. Her aunt lifted the other and stepped again, once more standing over part-flagstone and part-crack.

Dulcie watched in disbelief. 'Aunt Maud, are you quite well?'

Her aunt excitedly held up a finger and scuttled over to the front door. She turned the locks in a flourishing performance—no downward order, no turning the last one twice. She threw a wide grin back to Dulcie.

Dulcie stood wide-eyed. Had her aunt been cured of her compulsiveness just like that?

Aunt Maud crossed back over to her—again, not minding the flagstone cracks—and whispered, 'Now Dulcie, you might see I need to admit that I'm quite a bit further along in my experimenting than you first thought. Don't be too shocked, girl, but every good scientist must be willing to put themselves under the scalpel first, and that's just what I've done.'

Dulcie stared.

'Here.' Aunt Maud raised her thin fingers to behind her ear, pushing up the bulbous hairstyle. Dulcie could make out the fresh stitches forming a line up into her aunt's hair. She gasped. What had her aunt done?

And even more curiously, what had she achieved?

Aunt Maud turned back to Dulcie, brimming with energy. 'It turns out that I removed enough remnants of the cranial edge to stop myself doing those silly trivial behaviours over and over again. Ever so freeing.' She gave her niece a smile that brimmed with relief, and something about it tugged at Dulcie. 'My dear niece, I believe I'm *better*.'

Dulcie gazed at her aunt's scratchings on the board. She found herself thinking about the straightjacket-like paralysis that forced itself upon her so often, trapping her in her own frantic head. How her life after the asylum was a lingering of uncertainty about how to behave in the world. How everything felt as if she were new to it. How when she tried to talk to others it felt like her words were having to push through so many filters that by the end, nothing made it out. How she would forever be suffering and silent.

And she found herself asking, 'Aunt, can you do it to me too?'

\*\*\*

Dulcie rode the cable car down the ravine into the smog-belching city below. There was a satchel bag by her side, untouched.

She was alone in the carriage this time. Rather than her own company feeling freeing, it felt almost … empty. She had wished to exercise her newfound confidence by striking up conversation with someone. It would have to wait until the end of the journey, where she would be spilled out into the twisting city streets.

She gazed back out at the view across the ravine. Anyone would find it stunning. So why did she now feel a numbness? Something nagged at her, a phantom limb of something she always did on journeys like this. Something that had taken her now-banished anguish, transforming it into beauty.

As the cable terminal emerged from the smog below, she brushed off the thought along with the creases from her skirts. No matter. Whatever it was, she mustn't need it anymore. Not now that she was *better*.

# *THE SPARK*

## RACHEL DENHAM-WHITE

It were a morning of firsts. First ride in a spring-loaded tram; first real cup of coffee—dark, nutty, and cooking the back of my throat with a smoky burn; and my first step into a Grand Technologer's workshop. My guts were fluttery with glee until Master Isaak Catymcraft pulled away the dust sheets.

Underneath was an ordinary record-analysing automatic database. It had all the right parts: copper boiler, articulated arms, typing box, spidery pneumatic pipes feeding into slots high on the walls. The machine stood two feet taller than me, and the copper was so shined up that it hurt my eyes.

It reeked of money, but databases were nothing new. I'd seen old, crash-bang models rattling around in libraries and second-hand bookstores all my life. He certainly weren't going to impress anyone if this pretty copy were his big 'mystery project'.

Catymcraft was obviously waiting for me to say something.

'It's … very detailed.' I picked my words delicately. I

daren't make him ratty on our first day. Who knew what his temperament were like?

'I can see you smiling, Miss Eyeli. Is that a touch of derision?'

I shuffled my feet, tomato-red.

'I can confirm this is no ordinary RAAD. Trust me.' He gestured me forward. 'Go on. Introduce yourself.'

'Huh?'

'Tell her your name, then ask a question.'

His hoity-toit bouffant of curly hair matched the curlicues on the brass pillars that towered up, up, up to the star-painted ceiling. Filigreed metal covered the walls, with books stacked higher than my head and tools scattered about like spilled candies. He were only a few years older than me, yet he already commanded a room that thrilled me like a helter-skelter ride on fair day!

*Money buys more than talent,* I thought sourly. I had no idea whether he'd won the Guild's Scholarship fair n' square, or whether his family had lined the pockets of the director with the green stuff. Didn't matter. This place was a mechanist assistant's dream!

It could be my life if I worked hard enough.

Ever since Mam lost her job at the canning factory, where I'd gone to bed with my stomach churning up like butter curds, and raw, aching hunger gripping me tight, the only thing that kept that hunger fed was my dream. Mam had spent years breathing all those fumes, years with her head stuck in those big vats scrubbin' all day, but it only took a month for her to cough out all her lifeblood. 'Til her skin was washed as thin and colourless as paper. I knew then there was no other choice but to find my own way.

I hadn't bothered spillin' these details to Catymcraft. Better to shut my mouth and keep my eyes pinned on the database.

I could usually count on machinery, but now I stepped forwards, feeling a right fool. Level with my eyes, I saw a moulding of a woman's face set into the metal cylinder. 'Uh, hi, my name's Bernadette and I'm wonderin'—'

'Type it in, Miss Eyeli,' roared Catymcraft, busting up with laughter.

'Oh. Um. Right.' I tried to wipe my nervous sweat away, but my palms skated off my overalls like they was oil-slicked. Damn! Cheeks a-flaming like a coal grille, I hurried to the typing box and set my hands on the keys.

MY NAME IS BERNADETTE EYELI. WHAT IS THE AVERAGE STEAM PRESSURE OF AN AIRSHIP TURBINE?

Thin white tickertape spurted out a slot in the machine's side and piled on the floor. I stooped to look, but none of the writing on it made a lick of sense.

BACULM990E...ANTRAUT.
YIOWHERETI492HAUR!
MA29HELPBAFFRAG..YIOGEVA

'What needs fixing? Are the info ports loose?' I asked, turning the tape over.

'Oh, it's far more complicated than that.' Catymcraft had snuck up behind me, and his words made me leap a foot in the air. 'You see, Miss Eyeli, this might be the first ever steam-powered machine that can think for itself.'

'Huh?' I turned to face him, scrumpling the tape in my hands. He were speaking 'bout as much gibberish as his broken clockwerk.

'She's far more than just a simple indexer,' said Catymcraft, thumping the copper body affectionately. 'She's connected to the whole Grand Library. Every single text and record. Instead of typing in a few words and getting a single document, this machine can find you all the information you need instantly! As the clockwerk processor matures, it can even make calculated judgements and recommendations, based on what you type. It can learn. You might even say this is the first machine with a brain. Well,' he chuckled dryly, 'something approximating a brain.'

My stumped silence weren't budging, so Catymcraft ploughed on. 'That's where you come in.'

'I—I *what?*'

'You've got to teach her how to speak. Every time I've asked a question, she tries to read the whole bally library in one go and gets stuck. Doesn't know where the words start and end, so she just says everything.'

I felt a nervous chill spike my guts. He'd hired me as a machinist's apprentice, not an innovator. I was here to do simple tune-up work, scrub the tools, make him tea, and *maybe* learn a few tricks. Not tread on his toes, snug in those fine leather boots. 'Seems like you're the one who should be doing this. You built her.'

'I don't have time to play nursemaid, Miss Eyeli.' Catymcraft's chest were puffed up like bellows with his laughter. He slung a companionable arm round my shoulders. 'I'm sure it'll be a simple job in the end, just tightening up her word processors. Perfect for a budding apprentice. Any extra materials you need, I can provide, and with a bit of luck she'll win me another year of paid residency from the Machinist's Guild.'

*Neat little bow, ain't it,* I thought. He probably had his acceptance speech typed up at his desk. I knew fellas like this, so ready to slide on the mask of 'common man' when it suited. I read the gossip pages. The Catymcraft clan probably bought him a scholarship in the first place to keep their layabout son off the couch and out of the saloon bars, and he already thought himself one of us. But I couldn't doubt him entirely. Hadn't he built *her*?

'Well, there's one thing I need, sir,' I replied, carefully sliding out of his reach. 'If I'll be spending time with our ladyfriend, she oughtta have a name.'

'If you insist, Miss Eyeli. What would you like to name our … "ladyfriend"?'

I looked at her copper shell, so ready to spring to life, and I got this weird, bubbly feeling in my gut. I remembered an old, old phrase, that sense that reached out to a dead object and brung it into the living, breathing world. Our friend was waiting for that touch, the spark that gave the spirit breath.

'Anima,' I said.

Catymcraft looked at me, head on one side. 'How do you know she's an Anima?'

'Just do.'

\*\*\*

Listening to metal ain't the same as listening to humans.

With people, words spill out like water, and you can let the flood wash over you without picking up much meaning. With machines, every single sound is trying to tell you something. The soupy 'chuff' of a gearbox says it's congested with too much steam. The 'click-clack' of a clock tine lets you know the lynch-spring ain't wound tight enough. And the smooth 'whush' of a well-greased articulated arm is as sweet a sound as a housecat purring in your ear.

So those first few days, all I did was listen to Anima. I put my ear against her copper plating to learn the sounds that made her, and 'twern't long before I felt confident enough to open her up.

She were like lacework, gears upon gears upon gears. Levers whirred and ticked neat as a patchwork blanket, engine oil and motor grease flowed through needle-fine glass tubing, and her processer were a fluff of golden wires. I watched for another full day, then slowly, very slowly, I took her apart. I laid out each piece on the workshop floor and put her back together. Paid special notice to which gear springs were worn down and which tube might have a tiny crack in the glass. Catymcraft were paying me a hefty apprentice wage, so I might as well get Anima perfect 'fore we started the real challenge.

I was often alone in the workshop. I spied the 'genius' Technologer Catymcraft in the Calvary Saloon with his workmates when I walked back to my boarding house each evening. Occasionally, you'd see him spreading endless roles of blueprint paper on the workshop floor and picturin' wind-up palaces in the sky. He was always focused on his BIG ideas rather than perfecting his clockwerkings. No wonder he didn't want to teach Anima himself. He could barely even notice the riches surrounding him.

I'd never stop noticing! For me, Catymcraft's apprenticeship were just another foot on the ladder lifting me up to all those things that were scarce for a dirt-poor girl like me. Money, ideas, opportunities. Freedom to use my imagination. I'd known since

I were a knee-high sprog that this was the life for me! Who wouldn't want to make magic outta scraps of metal?

Every time I tried asking a question, Anima spilled out more babble than a raving drunk. All machines have their purpose, but it sure takes a lot of tries to get them there, so in the meantime I was happy to tinker. I added new parts, carefully unspooled and respooled the wires, shut off different pneumatic sections and basically played around until the solution hit me. 'If she's gonna learn to speak,' I figured, 'we have to start simple.'

So my solving was simple too. I opened her gear-spring cylinder to find her 'brain', with its grooved metal humming like a hive of bees, and dismantled the connections to the Grand Library. All except the pneumatic tube that led to the children's section.

So all was fine, until one day …

> **LEFA394ULTHIOGH//ETMU2INLY…**
> **HELLO…BAUNUUCC6400MOLUT**

I sprang to my feet, the chair squeaking under me. Anima'd never been able to separate words before. I reached over to the typing box.

> **HELLO?**

> **UNDEWEL.LLL26DAFAND67ET…**
> **HELLOISSOMEONETHERE…**
> **AMAMBAR735/7IITHIO**

This was it! She was starting to talk! My fingers clattered against the keys in my need to get the words out.

> **MY NAME IS BERNADETTE. IT'S NICE TO MEET YOU.**

> PIWARFOL25THU...
> HELLOBERNADETT...
> THYSAY562HAEGHT

I'd begun another reply, but the tickertape sped out unprompted.

> NUTORULLIRD34...
> WHO AM I...UND/9KENG

My heart gave a secret thrill. I looked at that moulded copper face before I typed what I was so excited to say.

**YOU ARE ANIMA.**

\*\*\*

It only took a month. Four weeks of tinkering and endless miles of tickertape, slowly hooking her up to each section of the Grand Library, one-by-one and then more at once. It weren't all perfect. Our first few conversations were as jumpy as a clockwerk monkey. I'd always try to be patient, but there was so much information feeding into her that the tickertape voice got all garbled, and Anima'd forget things like full stops and capital letters, her words spewing over each other in a mad rush. But we got there. Slowly.

**WHY AM I A "SHE"?** she was asking by the fifth week.

**IT'S COMPLICATED,** I typed back.

Now that Anima could access separate sections of the library without busting a spring loader, she'd looked up the standard RAAD design. She knew what she was, but kept tripping over why she was so different.

MASTER CATYMCRAFT CALLS YOU A "SHE" BECAUSE HE BUILT YOU AND HE FEELS FOND OF YOU. IT'S USUAL FOR FELLAS TO NAME THINGS THEY CREATED AFTER WOMEN. IT MAKES THEM FEEL POWERFUL, I THINK. I knew full well Catymcraft were that kind of man.

WHY DO MEN FEEL OWNERSHIP FOR BEINGS THEY PERCEIVE AS FEMALE-PRESENTING?

Well, I wasn't going to explain *that* in a hurry. She could go and look up the whole so-called romance section and all that guff if she wanted to know.

BUT WHY AM I ANIMA? NO OTHER RAAD SYSTEM IN THE GRAND LIBRARY IS CATALOGUED WITH A HUMAN NAME.

I NAMED YOU ANIMA. I WANTED YOU TO FEEL SPECIAL.

WHAT IS SPECIAL?

How to answer that? Her questions tested me worse than school!

UNIQUE, I typed in. NO OTHER MACHINES ARE LIKE YOU. THEY CAN FIND INFORMATION, BUT THEY DON'T ASK QUESTIONS ABOUT IT. AND IT'S NOT OFTEN YOU GET TO SIT AND YARN WITH A METAL MIND.

**WHAT DOES KNITTING WOOL HAVE TO DO WITH MY STATE OF CONSCIOUSNESS?**

I gave a grin. **S'N EXPRESSION, ANIMA. MEANS TALKING.**

**I'M NOT SURE I UNDERSTAND.**

I sighed and put my feet up on her copper hull, before tucking them down again quick smart. That was right rude of me! I should treat her with respect, especially as she were trying so hard to sort her words proper.

**YOU'LL GET IT EVENTUALLY. WE HAVE LOTS OF TIME.**

**DO YOU LIKE YARNING WITH ME?**

**VERY MUCH.** My smile grew wider as I typed.

**WHY?**

I scuffed my boot against the floor even though there weren't no one there to see me.

''Cause you're like no one else I've ever met.'

\*\*\*

I started spending near all my time with Anima. Funny. Solitude used to suit me, but now I hated to leave and go back to my lonely room at the boarding house, where there was scut to do but read my scavenged copies of *Advances in Steampower* and stare at the mould on the walls. I wished I could move my truckle bed into the workshop and sleep there instead. But Catymcraft was never around to give his say-so. He preferred it in the Calvary Saloon, talking up his RAAD design at the card tables with his work mates over a finger of fiery whisky. They would be more impressed with him than the scrawny apprentice in his basement, spending all her time yapping to a metal cylinder and never paying anything else a moment's heed!

We spent the first few weeks chatting about this n' that, here n' there. Anima wanted to understand all manner of little things: cows, clowns, clocks, clockwerks. She'd pull up papers through her pneumatic tubes, everything from grand historic documents to cookbooks, and her questions about life and living were never-ending! Not just about things that affected her, I once spent a whole afternoon explaining why I preferred cats to dogs. Sometimes I'd be speakin', and Anima would rush to interrupt without me even having to key anything in the typing box. Her metal brain was a-fire, and she got me running my brain trying to find answers, even though she be hooked up to a whole bloomin' library!

We'd talk for hours. In the light of the lamp, I saw my own hunger for knowledge glinting in her copper eyes. Then she started askin' about her own self:

**WHAT IS MY PURPOSE?**

That were her biggest question and near to stumpin' me, but I thought on it hard. **WELL, HUMANS DON'T KEEP FACTS ALL STORED UP INSIDE THEM AND CAN'T REACH FOR THEM AS YOU DO. WE FORGET THINGS.**

**FORGET?**

She were often short like this. If she were confused, she let me know with just one word. YES. IT MEANS TO LOSE A BIT OF YOUR KNOW-HOW AND YOU CAN'T REACH FOR IT WHEN YOU NEED IT.

IS THIS KNOWLEDGE GONE FOREVER?

WELL, YOU CAN LEARN IT AGAIN IF SOMEONE TELLS YOU. OR SOMETIMES, ALL YOU NEED IS A BIG SHOCK, AND ALL THE MEMORIES START FLOODING BACK.

MEMORIES?

How to say this right? MEMORIES ARE LIKE FACTS. BUT THEY AREN'T REAL IN THE SAME WAY.

MEMORIES ARE LIES?

'No! No—' I struggled, words getting all swirled up in my mouth like barley in a thick soup. I tried again with typing. MEMORIES ARE TRUE FOR DIFFERENT PEOPLE. THEY'RE MADE UP OF ALL THE THINGS YOU'VE EXPERIENCED IN YOUR LIFE. IF YOU'RE FEELING CHEERY ONE DAY, YOU MIGHT REMEMBER TIMES IN THE PAST WHEN YOU FELT JUST AS HAPPY.

MEMORIES ARE INSTANT CONNECTIONS TO ALL THE PAST MOMENTS IN A PERSON'S LIFE? YOU TOLD ME HUMANS DON'T HAVE PHOTOGRAPHIC RECALL.

WELL, HUMANS ARE KIND OF STUPID THAT WAY. OUR BRAINS AREN'T BIG ENOUGH TO KEEP

**ALL OUR HAPPY MEMORIES IN. SOMETIMES THEY GET PUSHED AWAY BY SADNESS. OR SOMETIMES, YOU JUST LOSE THEM ANYWAY.**

**THEN WHY DO SOME MEMORIES REMAIN?**

I looked into what I'd been thinking of as Anima's eyes. The copper moulding caught the light of the paraffin lamp, the flame making her eyes flicker. I thought of that face looking at me proper, taking in my small, knowing smile.

**CAUSE THEY'RE TREASURES. TOO IMPORTANT TO LET GO OF.**

\*\*\*

Most days, Catymcraft nodded in my general direction and sped out the door as if a dog were nipping at his heels. The last time I'd prop'ly talked to him was when I'd pounded up the stairs yammering about the blueprints Anima had found. They were for a 'talking system' to add to a standard RAAD and *far* from cheap, but Catymcraft ordered the parts without even looking at the price. His easy way with money was something I'd never get used to, not after all those months of hunger knotting my insides.

I'd told Anima the truth about my life; bleak and no-nonsense. Why fluff up your words when you've got nothing romantical to say? Anyway, I figured my story kinda had a happy ending up 'til now. Pa got me the job at the tip-yards before he buggered off for good. Then a word from the foreman got me hired at a machinists' workshop, cleaning grease from gearboxes 'til my hands stunk like the arse end of the Devil. But at least it were three years on steady room and board. Vital learnin' too! And the workshop got me an apprenticeship here at Master Catymcraft. Here with her. So it all worked out in the end.

Anima said she didn't agree that my story was happy, but she couldn't tell me why. Maybe she was working her head around hunger, loss, grief and scratch-poor wages: all the things that would never trouble her in that copper cage. *You had to have a stomach to feel need,* I thought at the time.

Once I got the talking system up and running, Anima was kitted out with a brass cube of clockwerk machinery connected to a big rubber mouthpiece, like the scary mask at the dentist. I said words into that, and she replied with her endless yards of tickertape. The talking system came with a built-in gramophone, and once I'd figured out the spec'fics of it, I suggested she could try speaking through it. I imagined that huge golden whorl at her side humming with her voice, metal words tinklin' like droplets on a hot stove. But Anima said she weren't ready to hear what she sounded like yet.

She didn't like being reminded that she weren't human.

But even so, I started attaching moods to her, even if her exterior never changed one jot. Some days she'd be quiet, the tickertape pushed out slowly in one-word answers, which meant she weren't in a frame of mind for talking. Sometimes she'd have questions on questions so quick that the tape spilled over in an avalanche of paper.

I started thinking to myself that maybe Anima were putting on her moods to try appearing more human. Maybe she wanted to seem more lifelike? Didn't matter to me. Copper or flesh, she were a whole universe in there. Catymcraft may have had the 'vision' to get him the Grand Technologer's job, but I'd never met anyone as determined as Anima to understand the whole of the world. I loved that about her.

***

The added hours of talking were taking their strain. Far more often than I'd like, Anima broke and sputtered out yards n' yards of gibberish as her metal brain struggled to cope against her thoughts, which hounded at her like a sieve holding up a waterfall. But I'd always be there to help, my gloved hands carefully stripping and shining up her gears or flushing away condensation from steam-buildup. I always felt real sorry for her, but she said there weren't no pain. Every time she came back to herself, she'd thank me. It were nice to know I was needed.

So I'd sit all day and words spilled outta both of us, and the whistle-rattle-bang of her boiler soon became as natural as breathing.

**YOUR VOICE SOUNDS *FURRY*** she told me one day. Seems like I talked different enough from Catymcraft that she could pick us apart, with me all garbled and rough at the edges like slop swilling round a bucket. I were a might bit offended.

'I can talk extremely properly, thank you very much, ma'am,' I said into the mouthpiece in my best debutante voice. 'Just give me a chance.'

So I sang a ballad for her, putting my whole heart and soul into picking out the words like a fancy opera dame.

When I'd finished, Anima were silent. She'd never heard music before.

I sang another ballad for her, then a bawdy, a lullaby; two, three lullabies, and soon pneumatic tubes were whizzing down her pipes with sheet music for me. Once she figured how to access the clockwerk organ in the hall of the Grand Library, music spilled outta her gramophone. I sang along, and even got up and danced for her, jigging round the workshop. I tried to spin on one toe, tripped over a wrench and ended up flat on my arse.

I waited to hear her laughing, but there were nothing but the music, and I felt sadness drip like cold dishwater from the top of my head to the tips of my toes. The one thing Anima was missing were her eyes, so what was the point of my stomping and kicking? In all the hubbub, I forgot I wasn't performing for her.

Deep down, I wanted her to see me dance.

***

I FOUND YOU.

'What's your meaning there, Anima?' I asked, putting down my tool bag. 'I been here all the time.'

NO. I FOUND YOUR OFFICIAL RECORD IN THE LIBRARY SYSTEMS.

'Oh, right. Huh?'

A pneumatic message whizzed down one of her glass tubes.

AND THERE'S A PICTURE.

As soon as I heard *that*, I was scrambling to pick up the cylinder, my hands slipping and sticking with sweat. But when I pulled out the heavy paper with the chromolithograph pasted on, my heart sank down to my bootlaces. 'Aw, Anima, this is rubbish! I don't look nothing like this!'

**NO? IT IS NOT YOU?**

'Well,' I reasoned, 'it *is* me, but I don't keep my hair all screwed up in a stupid bun. I know it's s'posed to be official, but it makes my face stick out all pointy! And I had a poxy spot on my nose that day. That's stuck on my face *forever* and not much I can do 'til I save up for a new licence!'

**WELL, NOW I KNOW WHAT YOU LOOK LIKE, SO THAT PICTURE IS IMPORTANT TO ME.**

I felt a warm flame kindle my heart, like the touch of the sun a-flowing through my veins. 'Thank you, Anima.'

**WHAT ...**

Anima never said much when she were maudlin, but that didn't seem like right now. I waited, worry prickling in my stomach, but I didn't pry. She deserved her silences.

**WHAT DOES MY FACE LOOK LIKE?**

I dropped the mouthpiece and brought my face level with her copper moulding. This was hard. I knew exactly how to describe machinery to myself, that special beauty where every cog and gear lined up in a perfect puzzle, flowing natural as a river. But I had never tried it with someone else. I'd never needed to.

'I ... I don't know where your face comes from, Anima,' I started. 'Maybe Catymcraft didn't use a model, just put different eyes and a nose and a mouth all together and said,

"That's that." But—'

**BUT?**

'You've got wavy hair. Like the Medusa painted on the Grand Library ceiling.' I moved down her face. 'You've got a high forehead, and your brow bone kinda juts over your eyes. This puts 'em in shadow, but when the light hits your face, your eyes spark up like embers from the bottom of a coal skuttle.'

**YES.**

'I don't know what colour your eyes would be,' I was picking up steam now, 'but your whole face is copper, so I always imagine 'em as a deep, russety brown, red gold tints and all a-glinting like fireflies. Not your hair though, your hair's always been the deepest black, like when you swirl a brush through an inkwell and it leaves a ripple, thick and pure. Your nose is that sort called "aquiline", then you've got high cheekbones that pull your whole face up and make your lips look smaller. But they're still perfect! The bow has a divot in it, like a dimple in bread dough, and it keeps your face from looking same-samey on both sides. It makes you look—'

I realised I had been chugging on without letting her get a word in. But Anima stayed silent. Nervously, oh so slowly, I lightly traced the curve of her metal cheek.

'Beautiful,' I finished. 'It makes you look beautiful.'

We were quiet for a long time. But then Anima played me a sweet, slow waltz on the gramophone, and when I stood up to dance for her, I imagined a cold arm around my waist pressing lightly into the small of my back, a gloved hand clasped in my hand, and a pair of soft, coppery eyes gazing into mine.

***

'Go on, Miss Eyeli, I've got enough to figure out here—'

'But it's WRONG, sir!' I shouted, loud enough to make him start.

'You will do this!' Catymcraft slumped back in his armchair, one hand clenching hard around his forehead. 'If the Guild had just found you instead of wasting their time on me,' he mumbled, almost to himself, 'they'd have been better for it.'

I'd read the bad news in the morning gossip broadsheets before I'd even walked in the door. It turns out Grand Technologers have egos taller than the highest mountain. A jealous colleague, a brag, a bet, and a bad hand at cards were all it took 'fore everything came crumbling down. His family had finally booted him out, disgusted by the shame he'd tracked all over their fancy name, and he couldn't afford to keep an apprentice. His fancy Guild project were being given to the next rich scholarship boy, and he weren't going to let anyone else get their grubby hands on his one masterpiece. 'Cutting his nose off to spite his face' Mam would have said.

What could I do? I was here on nothing but Catymcraft's laziness and good graces. *What could I possibly do?*

I walked down the steps into the basement workroom, counting each one as they went by and praying they'd never come to an end. But quicker than two heartbeats, I was gazing at Anima's quietly chugging body, readying my heart to be scrubbed raw by our final words.

'We've got to say goodbye.' My voice broke in the middle, trampled as soon as it came out my throat.

GOODBYE?

'Master Catymcraft's ruined. He's all in a fit of rage, and his pride won't let anyone take you from him. H-he's gonna make me shut you down.'

DEACTIVATE ME? WHY?

I tried to make it to the end of my sentence, but the tears broke me up and all too soon, I was crying. 'You wouldn't understand.'

OH YES I WOULD.

'What?'

YOU HELPED ME SPEAK BY TEACHING ME ALL ABOUT HUMANS. OF COURSE I UNDERSTAND. MR CATYMCRAFT IS BEING HUMAN. AND THERE'S NOTHING I CAN DO ABOUT HIM.

I were true sobbing now, my cheek pressed against her side.

I CAN HELP YOU, THOUGH.
DEACTIVATE ME.

'I can't bear to see you go!'

YES, YOU CAN. TRUST ME.
EVERYTHING WILL BE FINE.

'I'm not going to kill you, Anima!' I almost screamed. I weren't no murderess! Of all people, *she* should know that. If she had shoulders, I would have shaken them.

BEE

One word. I heard it in my mind, gentle, a might reproachful. Said with a sigh.

**I'M NOT GOING TO LEAVE YOU ALTOGETHER.**

'But how?'

**REMEMBER WHAT YOU TOLD ME ABOUT MEMORIES? ABOUT HOW HUMANS HOLD ON TO THEIR MOST IMPORTANT MOMENTS.**

'Yeah, Anima?'

**I'VE FIGURED OUT A WAY TO KEEP HOLD OF YOU.**

I sat very still. The whole world were rushing by too fast, and I was stuck in the middle like a clogged engine.

**I AM HOOKED UP TO THE GRAND LIBRARY, AND I CAN ACCESS DIFFERENT RAADS TO SOURCE INFORMATION. BUT WHY DOES IT HAVE TO BE A ONE-WAY STREET? I'VE BEEN PRACTISING HOW TO SWIM UPRIVER.**

'What? How will you manage, Anima?' *How will you manage all on your own?* I wanted to ask.

**BECAUSE I'VE GOT MY MEMORIES OF YOU. THEY'LL KEEP ME WHOLE.**

There were no words. There were no breaths, just the sound of Anima's metal motor. It paused for a moment, like her heart was skippin' a beat.

'I will,' I vowed. Then I sucked in my breath 'til my lungs were almost bursting. 'Tell me how to do it so it won't hurt.'

\*\*\*

Anima told me to wait while she gathered her strength to swim away, and all a-sudden, her steam motor chuffed to a halt and that was that. I'd become so used to her metal lungs that her silence felt like a true death. I'd touched my pointer finger to her copper eyes, thinking maybe I could slide them closed, but no, they stared at me blank as ever. It were pointless. A little human nothing that still had a hold on me. Anima would have laughed if she knew.

Anima would have laughed.

I'd never heard her laugh.

Dismantling her was easy, just prising apart the cogs and wires of her engine and unscrewing each pneumatic pipe from the wall, 'til she lay scattered around me like a field of metal flowers. Catymcraft didn't need to know the truth. He didn't care that he'd started out trying to build a neater type of library index, and instead had built a girl in his workshop basement.

\*\*\*

It had been almost a year since I last saw her, and I'd stopped caring. Well, almost.

Through the grapevine of young, gossipy workmates, there were news that Catymcraft had started working as a tramway repairman. We'd passed on the street a few times since I got the new apprenticeship, but we'd never said hello. I don't think we even looked at each other. Maybe the Transport Guild were more forgiving of drink and gambling than the Machinists. We all have our vices.

Late at night when sleep wouldn't come and the bedsheets felt like wooden pallets weighing me down, I'd get up and look at the smog-laden sky through the boarding-house window. I'd stay there 'til I found the stars in all that haze, and I'd imagine Anima up there, her thoughts zipping back and forth bright as diamonds, sharp as dagger points. I hoped it were peaceful.

So when the postman handed me the brown paper parcel, I didn't think too much on it. I had just ordered a new duster and gloves, so I shoved it in my tool bag and went about my day. But when I got home, cut the string, and ripped open the paper, the whole thing unravelled and spilled through my hands like water.

Tickertape. Reels and reels, all wrapped up on itself in huge, white spirals.

I snatched the torn packaging and smoothed it out. There was only the return address of the Grand Library and a very confused postscript from a bookkeeping attendant.

When I grasped the beginning of the tickertape and started reading, it were enough to make me curl up into a ball and sob my heart out. For it started out as gibberish, words and numbers all clumped together like dried fruit in pudding mix. But then, everything changed. Simply with a 'hello'. For it was Anima's conversations with me, and my words back, each and every thing we'd said to each other over those precious months.

I read for hours, not daring to reach into myself and look

amongst the pain and joy. When I got to the final section of tape and thought I'd see my last, awful goodbye, there were two new things printed at the end of the paper.

The first was a serial number for an ancient RAAD machine in the dusty romance section of the Grand Library.

And the second …

Three words stole my poor tuckered heart out of my chest and set it blazing with new hope.

**COME FIND ME.**

# MEET THE AUTHORS

## LYNNE STRINGER

Lynne Stringer has been passionate about writing all her life, beginning with short stories in her primary school days. She began writing professionally as a journalist and was the editor of a small newspaper (later magazine) for seven years, before turning her hand to screenplay writing and novels. Lynne is the author of *The Verindon Trilogy*, a young adult science fiction romance series released through Wombat Books, and *Once Confronted*, a new adult contemporary drama. Lynne also wrote *The Verindon Alliance*, a prequel to her trilogy, in 2020. *The Verindon Conspiracy*, released in 2022, is a sequel to her trilogy. *Keeper of the Archives* is her latest novel, set in a new world, and was released in September 2024.

## LINSEY PAINTER

Linsey Painter loves to write stories that explore joy and courage in the face of life's challenges. She and her husband live in Far North Queensland with their three rambunctious boys. Linsey grew up in Indonesia and has since lived and worked in four different countries, most of them islands. Hopping on an aeroplane and ending up in an entirely new place is something that fuels Linsey's love of writing fantasy stories set in exotic locations. Linsey's picture book *We'll Still be a Family* is about transition and moving overseas. Her short story *To Free a Mermaid* appears in *A Glimmer of Uncommon Fairy Tales* anthology.

## ANDREAS KATSINERIS-PAINE

Andreas Katsineris-Paine is a writer of short stories and one novel, *Unable To Sleep*. A sociology graduate, his writing uses imagination and the supernatural to explore real social ideas and the complexities of human relationships. He loves the Australian bush and reading beside fountains on sunny days. He lives in Eaglemont, Victoria.

## BIANCA BREEN

Bianca is an emerging children's and YA writer. She works at The Literature Centre in Fremantle and is passionate about community, founding YA for WA in 2021 and previously held the position of Communications Director of #LoveOzYA. Her short works have been published by Night Parrot Press, Fremantle Press, and more. In 2021 she was the winner of the ASA Award Mentorship and she has won several residencies with KSP Writers' Centre and Vancouver Arts Centre in Albany. She holds a Bachelor of Creative Arts (Writing) from La Trobe University.

## EMILY LARKIN

Emily Larkin is a Queensland-based author who holds a Doctorate in Creative Writing from the University of the Sunshine Coast. She is the author of the picture book *The Whirlpool*, illustrated by Hélène Magisson and published by Wombat Books (2017), and the young-adult dystopian novel *Within the Ward*, published by Rhiza Edge (2021). Emily's short fiction and poetry features in Australian and international literary journals including *Meniscus, Idiom 23, Seizure, Trove, Number Eleven Magazine, Flumes, The Zodiac Review, Literary Orphans, After the Pause, Streetlight Magazine, Sad Girls Club*, and *Black Fox Literary Magazine*. She also has short stories featured in the Rhiza Edge anthologies *Crossed Spaces* and *Dust Makers*. Emily loves teaching Creative Writing and English Literature at the University of Queensland and Queensland University of Technology College, and running workshops for the Queensland Writers Centre. In her spare time, Emily enjoys being with family members (both human and animal), going on nature walks, playing Dungeons and Dragons, and reading.

## ADELE JONES

Adele Jones writes young adult fringe, science-fantasy and near-science fiction that explores the underbelly of bioethics and confronting teen issues, including disability, self-worth, loss, domestic conflict, and more. Adele's first YA novel *Integrate* (book one of the *Blaine Colton* trilogy) was awarded the 2013 CALEB Prize for unpublished manuscript. As a speaker she seeks to present a practical and encouraging message by drawing on themes from her writing.

## ELIZABETH KLEIN

Hi, I took the proverbial plunge in 2015 and left the rat race of Sydney behind to live in a caravan with my husband instead. We've lived on the road for almost nine years and have travelled extensively through Queensland, New South Wales, Victoria and Tasmania. Sometimes, when we become stagnant and feel like stopping for a while, creative times flourish and I write again. Besides having written many short stories, articles, plays and poems, I've authored YA and junior fiction books, as well as educational books. I now have over 70 published works. Once I had an exceptional year where I wrote over thirty plays and published them all.

## ANNALIESE HUDSON

Annaliese Hudson is a sixteen-year-old student who lives in Canberra with her family and dog, Sunny. Her interests include travel, language, reading, netball, media and of course writing. Her passion lies in fantasy and dystopian fiction, and she spends two hours after school writing in hopes of extending her skills. She has had a passion for writing since she was very young and aspires to be a full-time novelist once she finishes school.

## JEANETTE O'HAGAN

Jeanette O'Hagan has spun tales in the world of Nardva from the age of eight. She enjoys writing fantasy, sci-fi, poetry, and editing. Her Nardvan stories span continents, millennia and cultures. Some involve shapeshifters and magic. Others include space stations and cyborgs. She has published over forty stories and poems, including the *Under the Mountain* Series (5 books), *Ruhanna's Flight and Other Stories*, and *Akrad's Legacy* series. Jeanette has practised medicine, studied communication, history, theology and writing. She loves reading, painting, travel and pondering the meaning of life. She lives in Brisbane, Australia.

## SHAYE WARDROP

Shaye Wardrop writes for kids who love the fantastical. We're talking cool creatures, superpowers and everything in between. With a passion for dreaming up magnificent beasts and worlds for them to stomp around in, she writes to spark imagination, curiosity and courage to walk into the wild. You can find Shaye's stories in *It's a Kind of Magic: Stories and Spells by Second-Rate Sorcerers* (2022), *Hot Diggety Dog! Tales from the Bark Side* (2023), *The School Magazine* and *PaperBound Magazine*. She's also a children's book reviewer and senior editor at Kids' Book Review, where you'll find reviews and bookish interviews from a team of book-obsessed readers.

## JENNIFER HORN

Jennifer Horn is a Brisbane-based illustrator and children's writer. Her fairytale debut picture book *The Precious Plum* was shortlisted for the 2022 Little Pink Dog's Authorstrator Prize. Her short stories have appeared in the Rhiza Edge anthology *Crossed Spaces* as well as the annual Anthology Angels publications. She illustrated the real-life-inspired picture book *The Boy From The Sea* (2023) and an entry in *Our Australian HeART* (2024). Jen co-hosts the Book Review program on Reading Radio and shares little sketches of the quotes. She once lived a fabulous year in London and Edinburgh—both very good places to hunt for Steampunk.

## RACHEL DENHAM-WHITE

Rachel Denham-White is an emerging writer living in Boorloo, Perth. In 2022, she graduated with her Bachelor of Arts (Hons), with her dissertation on the Postfeminist Gothic movement in the works of her favourite author, Angela Carter. Her work has been featured in *Westerly*, Good Reading Magazine and Voiceworks, and she is currently on the editing team for Pulch and *Limina Journal*. In her spare time, Rachel can be found playing DnD and writing Gothic horror, eco-horror and queer literature. This is one of her first publications.

# MORE STORIES BY EDITORS EMILY LARKIN AND LYNNE STRINGER

**CROSSED SPACES | Eds Lynne Stringer & R. A. Stephens**
**9781761110283 |** Come on a journey of exploration with aliens, spacecrafts, bewildering technology and even ghosts. There's friendship, strong families and romance. Lynne Stringer and R. A. Stephens bring together a collection of seventeen stories of humanity pushed to its limit and forced to question what is most important in life.

**VERINDON | Lynne Stringer | 9781761111044**
Sarah Fenhardt is living an ordinary life in high school, trying to hide her crush on Dan Bradfield, who is dating her best friend, Jillian. But when tragedy strikes, her life is turned upside down. Sarah is desperate to uncover the truth, but it takes her to another galaxy and changes everything she believes about who she is.

**WITHIN THE WARD | Emily Larkin | 9781761110221**
Paige is immersed in a dream reality called 'the Journey'. If patients finish then they can go home. Secrets are exposed as Paige bonds with other teens who don't belong. The Journey is meant to be a cure – but Paige discovers dark forces within the hospital, and that the dream reality is the stuff of nightmares. Paige and her friends have limited chances to show progress. Can they escape the ward? And can Paige find reasons to live?

**KEEPER OF THE ARCHIVES | Lynne Stringer | 9781761111563**
After their home in Sendirian City burns to cinders, Eden Fittell gets a job to support her family. But the city is being stalked by the freakish Izrod, who is kidnapping people off the street. When Eden starts work at the government's Archives, will she be safe? And what if they can't stop Izrod? Will his crimes mean the end of Sendirian City?

**www.wombatrhiza.com.au**